Deakins slipped off
reached into his flight suit.

Hale turned back. His gaze went from Deakin's narrowed eyes to a thin cylinder he was pulling from his suit.

"Jesus, Deak you can't smoke in – "

Hale bit off the rest of his sentence as Deakins pointed the cylinder at Hale's forehead. It wasn't a cigarette but the slender barrel of a Walther P38.

"Don't budge," Deakins said flatly.

"What do you mean?" Hale said.

Deakins said quietly, almost sadly, "I've decided, actually, to cash out now."

"Deak, you can't mean this. Come on, man. What the hell kind of joke is this?"

"No joke,' Deakins said. 'I'm sorry, partner. . ."

JEFF ROVIN

BROKEN ARROW

A novelisation by Jeff Rovin
Based on a screenplay by Graham Yost

HarperCollins*Publishers*

HarperCollins*Publishers*
77–85 Fulham Palace Road,
Hammersmith, London W6 8JB

This paperback edition 1996
Special overseas edition 1996
1 3 5 7 9 8 6 4 2

First published in the USA by
Boulevard Books, a division of the Berkley Publishing Group 1996
Published by arrangement with Twentieth Century Fox Licensing and
Merchandising, a unit of Fox, Inc.

Copyright © Twentieth Century Fox Film Corporation 1995

ISBN 0 00 649823 X

Set in Times

Printed and bound in Great Britain by
Caledonian International Book Manufacturing Ltd, Glasgow

When there is no peril in the fight,
there is no glory in the triumph.

—Pierre Corneille,
Le Cid

BROKEN ARROW

The gymnasium at Whiteman AFB, near the town of Knob Noster, Missouri, was brightly lit by rows of hanging fluorescent bulbs.

Too brightly lit, Vic Deakins thought as he circled his taller, ten-years-younger opponent.

Because of the glaring white light, Deakins could see every line, every sweaty hair, every diamond of perspiration on Reilly Hale's rugged face. He didn't *want* details like that. He wanted the whole man, the swarthy, almost muddy thing that flowed and danced and attacked. The living soul of the man. He had no use for these pieces, brightly delineated fragments that seemed less like a boxer than like a Halloween costume of one.

Beyond them, fliers and mechanics and desk jockeys were lifting weights and shooting baskets and doing their Tai Chi. Deakins saw them clearly, too, and hated their overly pumped and sharply defined shapes, their repetitive moves. They reminded him of blister-packed action figures.

This isn't the way it should be, Deakins thought.

When the Major was growing up in the Hell's Kitchen section of Manhattan, the gyms in which he hung out were real. They were for boxers only. You could practically feel the body odor, taste the sweat, hear the hearts bamming with rage. It was like the monkey house at the zoo, stinking and alive—not like this antiseptic temple of fitness, where the cardiovascular workouts were designed to get the blood flowing, not to build character.

The lighting back then was yellowish-to-dark, provided by a few dim bulbs hanging from long wires. Occasionally, they hissed as sweat from a bashed-back head or piledriver arm landed on them.

There are more dim bulbs in the rings than above them, Deakins thought fondly. And it was arguable which of them generated more wattage. But those guys had heart. Like the welterweight Bobby Prewitt, who was sharp and bloody as a razor. And smart. Years before Ali, he was playing mind games with his opponents. Then there was Dick C. Wells, a six-footer who had a spitfire left jab–right uppercut–left hook combo that could snap a head around like a tin can struck by buckshot.

But most of the palookas who got slammed into the sweat and blood–darkened corner cushions or occasionally got whomped against the ring posts were not smart, not fast, and not durable. After three rounds, their arms were twenty-pound buckwheat noodles hanging from their shoulders.

What they had, though, was a love of competition, and that gave them heart and drive and a little extra stamina that allowed them to look in the mirror afterward and call themselves men. The dignity that life beat out of them as they swept movie theater floors or hawked newspapers outside subway stops or stood in clouds of sizzling burger grease—they got that back here, in the ring.

Deakins loved all those guys, and he missed them. But most of all he missed the *times*. Not only were the gyms now sterile, but the people weren't athletes. They were clay, sculpted with the help of computer programs and steroids and vanity. And the ring was worst of all. The headgear and sissy mouthguards and protective cups were designed to take punishment the head and loins and soul used to endure, and an Air Force shrink stuck in her self-righteous pan now and then to make sure the sport of Jim Corbett and Rocky Marciano and the Sugar Rays Robinson and Leonard wasn't creating a race of mush-brained psychowarriors.

As if the world isn't doing that all by itself, Deakins thought as he faked right, then threw a brick-solid left at the unsuspecting Hale.

Hale's head had been moving to Deakins's left to escape the right. The left caught his cheekbone, stopped the face with an *oof,* and caused it to snap to the right. There, another of Deakins's rights was waiting. Only this one connected.

Landing a combo so fine brought Deakins's thoughts back to the ring, to this ring. He looked at Hale. With his short-cut black hair, round face, sharp ears, and narrow eyes, he reminded Deakins of an elf. One who wasn't too happy just now.

"Okay, you see what happened there?" Deakins asked with a Snidely Whiplash grin.

Hale shook his head several times. He looked like a sprinkler as sweat flew. "Pretty sure you hit me," Hale sputtered.

"Yeah, I hit you, Descartes," Deakins said, dancing on the balls of his feet. "Twice. You bleed, therefore you are. What happened was, I set you up. I forced you to move left, clocked you, then was free to use my right at my leisure. Result? *Rock 'em, Sock 'em Robot.*"

Deakins threw a right hook. Hale moved his head to the left, stopped as a left hook came screaming at him, and jerked right. He was nailed solidly by a right jab.

"Set you up again!" Deakins hooted, dancing higher now.

"Just call me Mr. Duckpin," Hale said.

"I'll call you slow on the uptake. See, you expect it again so instead I take the right in hard. That's what boxing's all about, friend. Make your opponent think you're gonna do one thing, then do another. Like Ali in Zaire, '74. Remember?"

3

"I was six, granpappy."

"Screw you," Deakins said. "Rent the videotape. Ali beat him using the rope-a-dope."

"The what?" Hale asked from behind his gloves.

Deakins lowered his arms. They swung with ape-like easiness at his side. He let his hairless chest deflate and his gut sag. His head bobbed from side to side.

"Hit me," Deakins said.

"Yeah, sure."

"Scout's honor," Deakins said. "I won't coldcock you. Try some kind of one-two."

Hale rolled his lips together, lowered his strong brow, and unleashed a feisty left uppercut. Deakins moved his head to the other side. When Hale followed with a right hook, Deakins pulled his hands in front of his face and took the blow in his gloves.

"See?" Deakins said, lowering his gloves. "You got a little worn down, and I got a chance to catch a breath. Just like in Zaire. Everyone thought Ali's arms were gone. Running on empty. En-oh—no. He was just letting Foreman wear himself out. Eighth round comes along, Ali starts hitting, George's got nothing left. Ding ding!"

"Fight's over," Hale said.

"You're learning," said Deakins.

Hale shifted his jaw from side to side. There was a look of consternation on his glistening features, as well as a loud popping from below his right ear.

"I'm also losing all feeling in the left side of my face," Hale complained. "That's okay, right?"

Deakins laughed. "It's what the new breed of pugilists calls 'Superficial shock re—'"

The front of Hale's left glove cut knocked the "action" back down Deakins's throat and snapped his head like a punching bag. A follow-up right caught him on the chin.

4

Deakins stepped back, his legs wobbly. He wasn't laughing anymore.

"You know what happened there?" Hale grinned. "You left me standing."

Deakins's angular features were cold, like a harrier eyeing its prey.

"Yeah," he said. His biceps tightened as he raised his arms. His fists moved in tiny, dangerous circles. "I won't make that mistake again."

Hale let out his belly and hunkered down behind his gloves. He breathed from his gut, not his chest, so he wouldn't lose his wind if his torso were hit.

"Don't waste your time with rope-a-dope," Deakins warned. "You aren't Ali."

Hale said nothing. He threw a left jab followed by a right uppercut. Deakins deflected the jab but the uppercut landed, albeit barely, as Deakins took a step back. He was still stepping back as Hale caught him flush with a left hook.

Deakins was hurt. He had to plant his feet firmly to remain standing.

Hale lowered his arms and sucked down a deep breath.

Before Hale could exhale, however, Deakins had recovered sufficiently to unleash a right uppercut that caused Hale to stagger back. Before Hale could recover, the shorter man moved in with a battery of uppercuts and crosses that put Hale behind his gloves and against the ropes.

Deakins grunted with each blow, oblivious to the crowd collecting around the ring, "woo-woo-wooing" with approval, some of them cheering Hale on. Lots of these folks didn't like Deakins, but Deakins didn't give a rat's hairy. Most of them had lost to him at poker, been passed over for flight assignments that he got, or got whupped by him right here in the ring. No one liked a winner, except the winner's mother.

Deakins closed in on Hale as he moved to the left, toward his corner. A right cross drew blood from Hale's left nostril.

"You're bleeding," Deakins crowed. "That's always the beginning of the end."

"Hey, Deak!" someone yelled. "Give him some breathing room!"

Deakins backed away, his fists circling quicker than before. Hale took a step in and raised his fists, though they weren't as high or as confident as they'd been.

"Let me give you a little tip," Deakins said, the hint of a smile returning. "Don't watch my hands. Watch my shoulders. That's where the punch starts."

Deakins illustrated with a right uppercut that sent perspiration spraying onto the turnbuckle pads.

"See what I mean?" Deakins asked.

Hale backed away, just two steps away from the corner cushions.

"You were looking at my hands," Deakins chided. "Let's try it again. Ready?"

Hale answered yes with his silence. Deakins faked with a left uppercut and connected with a right cross.

Hale fell back a step but remained standing. The hangdog expression was hanging more than before.

"Come on. Focus. Ready?" Deakins asked.

Deakins unleashed two fakes, a left cross and a right jab, and then the left hook connected.

"My shoulders," Deakins said. "That's how you tell the counterfeits from the real bills. Ready?"

Hale's eyebrows scrunched. The fabric of the gloves tightened on top as his fists did, and he nodded.

Deakins faked left. Hale's eyes were on Deakins's shoulders, and he didn't move. Hale saw a momentary opening and tried to take advantage of it with a right cross. Deakins was impressed, but he had enough room to jump back, out of the way, then step back in. As he did, he put everything into a right uppercut.

Hale was trapped, and from his *dammit* look Deakins could tell he knew it. Hale couldn't get his arm back and gloves up fast enough to protect himself; he looked like Yul Brynner watching the Red Sea close in on his charioteers. There was nothing to do but take what was coming. And what was coming was a right uppercut that started just above Deakins's knee and ended on Hale's mouth, like a kiss from a wrecking ball. Hale flopped back against the cushions, tried to hold onto the ropes with his gloves, but only succeeded in breaking his fall, not preventing it. Blood seeped from around the base of a tooth, pooled behind his lip, and spilled over the side.

Deakins stood over him, no longer angry. He motioned with a fist, and one of the other fighters climbed onto the apron and unlaced Deakins's glove.

He offered his hand to Hale, who pushed it aside. Deakins ignored him and helped him to his feet.

"The rule of the ring," Deakins said, "is that when the gloves come off, you leave the fight behind."

Hale leaned face-forward against the ropes as a soldier undid his laces. When the gloves were off, one of the jocks tossed Hale a sweaty towel, which he stuffed between his lower lip and his gum.

"It's behind," Hale said when he removed the towel. He pushed it back in for a moment, jabbed it around, then wiggled his tooth to make sure it was still secure. "Can I leave the pain behind, too?"

Deakins laughed as he helped Hale through the ropes. "Only when you die, my friend," Deakins said. "Only then."

2

The water pressure in the locker room was never strong enough to revitalize the sore skin, or hot enough to revive the deadened soul. But today, lukewarm and drizzly, it was just what Hale needed to wash out a battered mouth and soothe weary arms.

Once every week, for five months, Hale and Deakins had climbed into the ring. "To spar," as Deakins called it. And once a week Deakins gave him a lesson in the pugilistic arts. How to take a punch, why you don't stand flat-footed, how to protect your chin—all of it illustrated with blows.

Hale wasn't sure why he'd agreed to do it way back when, other than the fact that Deakins was a pal who needed a sparring partner and he gave him twenty-to-one odds on each fight. Besides, it was better to be sore than to have Deakins moping or edgy when they sat together in the cockpit. Still, right now he wondered why they couldn't play hoop or tennis like other fliers. Hale sucked at those, too, but a jammed thumb or fuzzy ball in the back of the head weren't as painful as this.

We do this because Deak likes to do what he's good at, Hale told himself. *He also likes to win.*

That was what made Deakins a great pilot. That was why he went into a serious funk when he failed to make the grade at the

Pentagon. And that was why Hale agreed to spar with him, to help bring him out of his depression. It seemed to be working, though Hale wondered if he'd have any teeth or discernible bone structure left by the time Deakins was cured.

Deakins had finished showering first. He was already suiting up on the bench, beneath a tester of cigarette smoke. Hale lumbered into the nearly deserted locker room, a towel around his waist. His trim but not overly muscular chest was red from a couple of body blows he'd taken early in the warm-up. They didn't hurt—not yet. That would come tomorrow. The pain always came later, like getting kicked in the nuts.

Though Hale had never given Deakins the combination, the door of his locker was opened, as usual. The inside was covered with photographs of exotic airplanes, from the SR-71 to the Super Mirage 4000; the only cheesecake pose was of supermodel Ruth Springer, and she was only there because of the F-117A on the tarmac behind her.

Deakins watched as Hale sat down and flopped an armful of clothes on the seat beside him.

"Jesus," Hale said, "do I have to watch you smoke right after you kick my ass?"

"Yep. Add insult to injury, son, that's my motto."

Hale waved through the smoke and glanced at Deakins's locker, which was spare and Zen-like in its neatness.

"You know what your lungs must look like?" Hale asked.

"Dark and nasty, like my soul," Deakins said. "Next time we're in an outta-control power dive, we can compare lungs. Like it'll matter, right?"

"Just 'cause we live dangerously, doesn't mean we have to screw up our bodies," Hale said. "Besides, you're not supposed to smoke in here."

"So I've heard," Deakins said. "What're you gonna do—beat me up?"

9

"One day I will," Hale vowed. He stretched his hand toward his partner. There was a twenty-dollar bill between his index and middle fingers. "In the meantime, here."

Deakins squinted through the smoke. "Nope. I can't accept that, bud. Not today."

Hale urged the money on him. "Just take it and shut up."

Deakins held up a hand. "No, really. I can't. I feel bad. How many times have we fought, and how many times have you won?"

"A gazillion, and never," Hale replied. "Come on. All I need's just two victories and I win it all back. Now take the money, jerk."

Deakins grinned. "If you insist." He folded the money into the front pocket of his flight suit.

Hale began dressing. His movements were slow.

"You know why I beat you?" Deakins asked.

"Because you've been boxing for twenty years and you're much better at it than I am?" Hale suggested.

Deakins shook his head. "Because you don't want it bad enough."

"Cow pucks," Hale said.

"No, really. You don't have the will to win."

Hale scowled. "Stop, Deak. Your deep insight is just too much for me to digest."

"Look, this is no shit," Deakins said. "You had me today. You clipped me with that right uppercut and then clocked me good with that left hook. I was back on my heels. You could have shut me down. But you blinked."

Hale rolled a shoulder. "We were just sparring."

Deakins's gaze hardened. "Uh-uh. Thinking that, that's why you lost. Life isn't about sparring, Hale."

"I think I saw that on a T-shirt once," Hale said.

Deakins shook his head. "You know what your problem is?"

"You just told me," Hale said as he bent to pull on his socks. "I don't want it bad enough."

"I don't mean about boxing," Deakins said. "Your problem is you don't fight for *anything*. Remember that waitress in Chow Fat's restaurant last week, Libby Charshee—"

"Yeah, but I wasn't her type," Hale said defensively. "She had tattoos of earrings on her earlobes."

"Steve Burkow wasn't her type either and she went out with him."

Hale looked surprised. "She did?"

Deakins nodded.

"Well, good for Steve," Hale said.

"Screwed him, too."

"Double-good."

"I hear it was. You also didn't take back that sixties CD you bought last week," Deakins said. "Bar code scanner didn't register the sale price—they owe you a buck. But you shrug it off."

"I've found bucks in the street," Hale said. "Way I see it, God evens things out."

"God's got better things to do than keep track of your finances," Deakins said. "You've got to look out for yourself. We all do."

"So you've got it all figured out, then," Hale said as he pulled on his flight suit. "Well, maybe you got it all wrong, Deak."

"I doubt it."

"Really? You ever think that maybe you fight too much?"

Deakins snickered. "There's no such thing as fighting *too* much. Bottom dog's got to fight to improve his lot, and even the top dog's got to fight to stay on top. Life *is* fighting."

"What about diplomacy?" Hale asked. "You'd be in the Pentagon today if you'd learned to bend a little. If you didn't insist on telling everyone exactly what it is they're doing

11

wrong. If every discussion didn't grow from debate to disagreement to fight."

"Admit it, though," Deakins said. "I'm usually right, aren't I?"

Hale made a face. "Pointing out screwups in the military doesn't exactly put you in the genius class, Deak."

"It isn't just the military," Deakins shot back. "The gym, Chow Fat's, the locker room—I'm right wherever I go." He took a long drag from his cigarette, then pulled out the twenty-dollar bill and handed it back to Hale. "Take this back."

Hale shook his head. "No. That's yours."

"If you weren't giving the fight everything you've got, then I don't want it."

"No," Hale said, "I mean—that's yours, literally. I took it from your locker just now."

Hale flung Deakins his wallet, and Deakins slumped forward, the cigarette hanging on his lower lip.

"Once in a while, partner, you *do* pull one out of a hat," Deakins said. He slipped the money into his wallet and put his wallet back in the locker. He closed the door and gave the tumblers a spin, then looked at his watch. "I'll give you another ninety seconds, then I'm off to the briefing. General Boone was acting a little cranky today, and I don't want to be late."

Hale zipped up the front of his charcoal-gray flight suit. As he laced up his black boots, he ran his tongue along his lower teeth. "The bleeding seems to have stopped. I think I can attend without spitting or making a spectacle of myself."

Deakins stood and lit a fresh cigarette with the old one. "Just once, I'd *like* to see you make a spectacle of yourself. Shuck off the inhibitions from your Texas youth, get drunk, play a CD-ROM porn game, tie your shoes one eyelet short of the top—something. Anything."

Hale finished lacing his boots and rose. The litany of his virtues made him feel better. "Flying at mach-two-plus is all the excitement I need, Deak. Maybe one day you'll learn to be satisfied with life's simpler rewards."

"I doubt that very much," Deakins said, slapping his partner on the back as they left the locker room.

3

If he had been twenty to thirty pounds lighter and twenty years younger, General Hubert "Dan'l" Boone would've been a dead ringer for Colin Clive in *Frankenstein*. Small nose, deep-set eyes, slicked-back hair—albeit grayish-brown, not Clive-black—a patrician air of superiority bordering on loathing.

Hale didn't know why, but he liked the sixty-year-old.

As Deakins and Hale walked in, Boone was sitting behind his big gunmetal desk, looking at a map on his computer screen. Two young aides were behind him, hunched over the screen.

"General," the fliers said, saluting.

"Evening, gentlemen," Boone said. He looked up and touched the side of an index finger to his forehead. His aides acknowledged the men with a nod, then did a Si and Am slink through a rear door into the small situation room.

I've got a secret and I'm not telling, Hale thought as he read their expressions. He didn't know whether to be worried or excited and ended up with a taste of both.

Boone's eyes settled on Deakins and remained there. "*Major,* is my name Rip Van Winkle?"

Deakins looked at him curiously. "Sir?"

"Have I been sleeping, and were you recently promoted past me?"

"Uh . . . no, sir," Deakins said.

Boone's eyes drifted to the red-and-white No Smoking sign on the wall. "Then why are you smoking in my briefing room?"

"Holy infraction!" Deakins said. He plucked the cigarette from his mouth. "May I?" he asked, leaning toward a Pentagon ashtray on the desk.

"No you may not," Boone replied. "I got that from Omar Bradley himself."

"Oops, sorry," Deakins said. He straightened, crushed the cigarette out between his thumb and index finger, and slipped the dead butt in his pocket.

Hale was wearing a *Didn't I warn you?* expression. The major shook his head.

"What's the mission profile, sir?" Deakins asked.

Boone sat back. "You're to simulate a low-level border penetration. Hug the ground."

"Scare some cows," Hale said, "and piss off some farmers, assuming they can spot you."

"The usual," Deakins said.

"Not exactly, Deak," Boone said. "Tonight it's going to be a little unusual. You'll be carrying a couple of nukes, gentlemen."

Hale and Deakins swapped looks. Hale's was one of disbelief, Deakins's one of delight.

"Real ones?" Hale asked.

"The genuine articles," Boone replied. "Palmdale's concerned about low-level gamma and X-ray diffusion screwing up the peripherals in the aircraft. So they asked us to send a couple on the run, see if anything lights up."

"Sixty-ones?" Hale asked.

Boone shook his head slowly. "Big ones."

"Eighty-threes," Deakins said.

Boone nodded.

"Oooh," Hale said. "Crowd pleasers."

"Yes," said Boone. His eyes fastened on Deakins. "And Deak?"

"Sir?"

"Do me a favor."

"Anything, sir."

"Don't give the security boys a hard time this afternoon."

Deakins appeared hurt. "Sir, I assure you I have a lot of respect for—"

"Save the bullshit for the waitresses at Chow Fat," Boone said.

"Yes, sir."

The general lifted a sheet of paper and shook it. Hale could see *Whiteman AFB Security/Eyes Only* printed in bold red letters across the top.

"I know about the Boogerman sticker you pasted on your ID yesterday, and the Michaelson's Gym membership card from 1968 you tried to pass off two days before that."

Deakins said, "I was just trying to keep things loose, sir. It can get a little hairy out there sometimes."

"I sympathize," Boone said. "And since you're also one of my best pilots, I'm going to overlook these complaints—"

"Thank you from the bottom," Deakins bowed slightly.

"—for now," the general added. "One more incident like these and I'm going to ground you for a month of Sundays. Got that?"

"Loud and clear, sir."

Boone shook his head. "I don't like to threaten a man of your caliber, but I don't run this base for your amusement."

"No, you certainly do not, sir."

Boone folded the paper and tore it in two. "Now, gentlemen— have yourselves a good fight and I'll see you on your return."

"Yes, sir," both men said, saluting.

"And thank you, sir," Deakins added. "Thank you very much."

Boone motioned him out with a wave of his hand.

As the men turned and left, Hale wondered whether Boone had tasted Deakins's insincerity beneath its thin candy shell, or if it were necessary to share a cockpit and adjoining lockers to read Deakins that well.

Or could it be denial? Hale wondered. Deakins was Boone's boy, handpicked seventeen years ago out of flight school and given all the juicy new planes. They'd been together ever since. The general didn't think bad thoughts about him unless he saw them in writing. And even then, as today, he cut him slack thick as a couple of time zones.

However, if Boone had been a little melancholy, Deakins was anything but. His step was jaunty as they headed through the outer office of the administration building, toward the field and the row of hangars.

4

The ghosts were everywhere.

Hale saw them, heard them, felt them. Beside him, Deakins was oblivious to the ghosts. But to Hale, they were like pterodactyls in the museum of his memory: the test planes that had flown here and at the other bases he'd been to.

There were pale shadows of the silver Bell X series of mach-breakers, the camouflage-green Boeing Stratofortresses, and the thundering, blue B-29s. He could hear the whoosh of the white Grumman F-14A Tomcats, the rumble of the ivory-gray Hawkeyes and Prowlers.

Ever since he was a kid in Texas, growing up with an uncle who worked for the space center in Houston, he wanted to go fast. First on horses, then in cars, finally in planes. He followed the space flights: the earliest he could remember was Apollo 7, in October of 1968, with Schirra, Eisele, and Cunningham onboard. But being an astronaut didn't seem hands-on enough for Reilly Hale. Even the launch, one of the gut-rumblingest and most powerful experiences to *watch*, was a spectator sport for the astronaut.

Hale wanted to control his vehicle. He wanted the excitement of riding *and* breaking the bronco. And fear? Of course it was there. The fear of screwing up. The fear of being maimed. But even if he'd ended up on his back, taking a long dirt nap, at least he'd have had the privilege of dying with his boots on. And that meant a lot.

Hale breathed in the mixture of fresh air and fuel. Even when he was flying solo, the smells and history and hardware all made him feel part of the community of fliers, an eternal brotherhood that not even death could take from him.

The bomb truck reached the hangar at the same time they did.

"Hey, Mike," Deakins said to the driver. "How's Meagan doing?"

"Better, Major," said the youthful airman in camouflage trousers and a brown T-shirt. "Baby's gaining weight, too."

"Glad to hear it," Deakins said. "Tell your wife hi for me, and give the baby a kiss."

The driver nodded and drove off.

"Nice guy," Deakins said. "And his wife's a real piece. Ever met Meg?"

"No," said Hale.

Deakins smacked his lips. "Quite a party girl in her day. Used to need three men to—"

"I don't want to hear it," Hale said. "You've got this remarkable talent for knowing the tawdriest things about people."

Deakins frowned. "Not tawdry. Exciting. Alive. There's nothing wrong with enjoying life, pard. Nothing at all."

Hale shook his head as they approached the sentry at the hangar door.

The hangar was new and modern, built as part of the expansive modernization program at Whiteman. Formerly the home of the Minuteman II and III missiles, it had been converted from 1988 to 1991 to handle the B-2A bomber and other Stealth aircraft—what the pros of the 509th Wing referred to as "low observables." Prior to the resurfacing of the runways and construction of six new hangars and support buildings, planes hadn't operated from the base since 1962.

The guard saluted, after which Deakins and Hale allowed her to examine their clip-on IDs.

Deakins grinned wryly as he wiggled his undefaced card at her. Hale gave him a *cut it out* look.

The sentry pulled a black device from a loop in her belt. It was the size of a remote control unit, and she checked the up-to-the-minute duty roster on the LCD display near the top.

"Go ahead, Captain Hale, Major Deakins," she said, saluting again, her own ID reflecting the sunlight.

"Thank you," Deakins said, returning the salute.

Hale entered first.

Light cascaded into the hangar as the large door was opened to admit the bomb truck. The sunlight rolled in, lighting the bomber from bottom to top, illuminating the red letters that spelled out *Spirit 7* on the inside of the bomb bay doors.

The Northrop B-3 was a black, flying wing even flatter and smoother than the B-2A. Though it had the familiar Double W trailing edge formation, the hatchet wings were swept back even further than the B-2A's thirty degrees, making for a smaller surface area, while the main fuselage was nearly a foot flatter. Unlike the B-2A, the nacelles were nearly flush with the wing surface, while the beaver tail and wing flaps had been redesigned to give greater lift and increase the bomber's range. In flight, in both the visual and radar spectrums, this plane was more than just low-observable. It was practically invisible. Hence the plane's nickname, the Ghost.

The bomb bay doors were open and the ground crew stood ready to load the cargo. Hale and Deakins greeted everyone with a hello and a smile; though Deakins's was the more velvety, both men carried themselves with the aloofness that became their status as crack test pilots—the warlike Ares, sun-drenched Apollo, and fleet Hermes—an Olympian hat trick packed tightly in one cockpit.

"You still got attitude," Hale said behind his smile. "Why is that, Deak? Why does everyone have to kiss your ass?"

"Because for twenty years I've been putting that ass on the line a couple times a week. It's golden, Hale. Solid, Sutter's Mill vintage gold ass. If, we get a glitch in some squat-sized chip in the stabilization augmentation system, and that ass is slag. So while it's whole, while it's mine, it deserves to be revered."

Hale said, "How come I take those same risks and don't feel the way you do?"

Deakins paused on the bottom of the crew entry steps, beside the cockpit, and looked back at his partner. "Because like I said before, you don't like to fight."

"And like I've told you before," Hale said, "if you've got to fight to show someone your ass is gold, then your cheeks must not be shining too bright."

"Not true," Deakins said. "Someone's got their back to the sun, you got to turn them around. They don't want to look, you've got to *pull* them around."

Hale shook his head. "I love you, but I don't know why we bother to talk about these things. Even with me, you fight. We just go round and round—"

"Hey," Deak said with a grin, "you think Patty and Cathy Lane got along all the time?"

"Who?"

"Cousins," Deakins said. "Identical cousins. Never mind."

While the bombs were being clamped into place in the rotary racks behind them, Deakins pulled on his helmet. Then he turned and hopped up the retractable silver ladder mounted to the left and rear of the nose wheel—five straight-up rungs into the cockpit. He pulled himself through the underbelly hatch

21

into the right-hand seat. Hale climbed into the left-hand seat, and as the hatch was closed the men strapped themselves in.

The cockpit was surprisingly roomy from side to side. The control stick and throttle quadrant were similar to those of conventional aircraft, and two large, angled, kite-shaped windscreens in front and two smaller rectangles on the side gave them a visual range of 270 degrees.

But the crew rarely used the windows. Flying the B-3 was done primarily via the four cathode-ray-tube multi-function displays arrayed in a T formation in front of each pilot, three on top and one underneath. The full-color screens provided duplicate information, left and right, about weather conditions, target data, radar readings, fuel consumption, and more. Topographic maps from above or straight-on could be brought up with the touch of a key.

Deakins was all business now. He and Hale went through the preflight checklist, ranging from cockpit pressurization and air conditioning to making sure the ACES II upward-firing ejection seats were armed and functional. They communicated with the tower, and when the bombs had been loaded the alarm horns sounded and the bomber was rolled out.

As Deakins guided the plane to the runway, Hale brought up the flight plan.

"So what's it to be? My guess is Wyoming."

Deakins glanced at the monitor. "Utah."

Hale smiled. "Well, it's about time. Damn Mormons with those TV commercials that make you feel guilty about yelling at your kids. Hell, yeah! Let's nuke the Beehive State!" He threw a tiny pair of left jabs toward the windscreen. "How's *that* for fight, pardner?"

Deakins grinned. "Real good, Hale. Real good."

Reaching the runway, Hale put his gloved hand atop Deakins's, which was on the throttle. Upon receiving a final go from the tower, they powered up the B-3 almost soundlessly.

Mounted in pairs in the center of the fuselage, outboard of the twin bomb bays, the four General Electric F118-GE-100 nonwaterburning engines poured out nineteen thousand pounds of thrust each. They were equipped with various Stealth systems which mixed the exhaust with surrounding air to disburse it, while contrail formation was minimized by chemicals fed into the exhaust stream. However, the pride of Northrop was the S-shaped inlet, which reduced to practically nil the engine compressor-face radar return.

As the bomber moved forward, the leading edges of the plane sliced cleanly through the air, their dielectric radar-absorbing material whispering defiance as they rose. Instead of climbing toward its maximum-tested height of forty-five thousand feet, Deakins guided the plane to just over half that altitude as it slashed toward the sinking sun.

5

A crescent moon was suspended in the blue-black sky. It hung like a Christmas ornament from the tallest of the group of junipers. One thousand feet below the trees, to the southeast, the Colorado River surged along the jagged course it had cut through the rock—rock that had provided scientists with some of the richest sources of uranium in the nation. Ninety miles southeast of that was the point where Utah, Arizona, Colorado, and New Mexico touched, the only place in the country where four states shared a common boundary.

Just beside the trees was an easel with a stretched canvas. The unfinished painting showed the river with the sun reflected in rippling dashes of yellow. Behind the painting was a dying campfire close to an Army surplus tent, and in the tent the artist, Jim Solomon, was snuggled close to his wife Wanda. Jim was newly retired from the arts pages of the Chicago *Tribune,* and the drive from the Windy City to Utah was their way of celebrating. They had arrived at sunset, eaten, and promptly collapsed in each other's arms, intending to make love, but Wanda had a cold and Jim was too tired from driving for even a run at the preliminaries.

Their packed Blazer sat several yards away, on the dirt road by the edge of the escarpment. Its chrome fenders and gray sides glinted as the headlights of a truck struck it; the lights were cut almost at once, though dirt still crunched as the tires passed over it, more slowly once the headlights were off.

The truck stopped some twenty yards away. The driver's side door opened, a flashlight snapped on, and the circle of light caught the green printing on the white door that read *Canyonlands National Park Rangers.*

The flashlight dropped a circle of light on the scrub and rock, and on the squeaky brown hiking boots and green cuffs of the ranger. He checked the inside of the car, front seat then back, before walking over to the tent. The fire threw orange waves across his uniform as he tapped on the ridgepole.

"Evening," he said loudly. "Park ranger. I'd like to talk to somebody about this fire."

Dark shapes moved inside the tent.

"Wha—?" said a man's voice, startled. "Oh, hell!"

A woman's voice said, "I'll talk to him, Jim."

"It's all right, Wanda," Jim replied sourly. "You stay put."

Jim hadn't bothered to zipper the door. He ducked out of the tent, still dressed, and held a hand palm-out to shield his eyes from the flashlight.

"Officer," he said, "or sir or—I'm not sure what to call you—"

"Ranger," said the voice.

"Ranger," said Jim, "I know we're not supposed to have wood fires in the park. It's the dry season, and there's lots of leaves and wood. It's just—Wanda's got a cold and I wanted her to stay warm."

The ranger began kicking it out with his shoe.

Jim watched as soot-sized embers flew up and about. "I'll get some water—"

"Sir," said the ranger, "have you seen any other hikers or campers anywhere around here?"

25

"Not this time of year," said Jim. "That's why we came here. They told me in Moab that it's dead now."

"True," said the ranger.

Jim rubbed his arms in the sudden cold. "What's the fine for something like this?"

"Pretty steep," the ranger said casually. "Your life."

Jim grinned. His mouth, like the moon, was a beaming crescent frozen in the glow of the flashlight. But the smile collapsed as he saw the shadowy shape of a .38-caliber pistol and silencer, and it twisted into something surreal as the ranger put three bullets into his heart. Jim fell onto the remnants of the fire, throwing up more sparks, and the ranger fired three more shots into the shadow of the woman sitting inside the tent. She flew backward, her feet thumping down in the open doorway, dark splotches spattering the inside of the tent.

The ranger unfastened the silencer, returned the gun to its holster, snapped off the flashlight, and took his walkie-talkie from its belt loop.

"Baker here," he said after switching on the transceiver.

"Go ahead," said a voice on the other end.

"Secured," Baker said.

"Very good," said the other voice.

A moment later, larger headlights washed over the campsite as a pair of Humvees rolled up the winding path. The big vehicles stopped behind the ranger truck.

The wiry passenger in the first Humvee, Novacek, left the walkie-talkie on the seat as he got out.

"I thought rangers are supposed to *preserve* our natural resources—like people," he said to Baker.

"Shut up and help me with Johnson's gear," said Lett, the gangly driver.

"Professor" Johnson, who had been driving the second Humvee, looked away from the carnage as the other two unloaded a large trunk from their vehicle.

"Don't take it like that," said a man who was still sitting inside the second Humvee. "Feel glad for them. How many people get to die quickly, painlessly, in such a tranquil setting?"

Johnson was facing the Humvee, his long-fingered hands splayed on top. "Somehow, Mr. Pritchett, that fails to console."

The slender figure cocked his head to one side in acquiescence. "Perhaps it falls a little short at that. In which case, think of money, Mr. Johnson. Lots of it."

"I'll try," Johnson replied.

"Good. Only, think of it while you work—there's a great deal to be done."

Nodding weakly, Johnson pushed his thick-rimmed glasses back on his nose, then walked to where the other men were opening the trunk, mercifully out of sight of the bodies.

"Oh, and Mr. Baker?" Pritchett called.

"Yo!"

"Drag nature boy from the fire, or we'll be smelling him all night."

"Roger," Baker said.

The killer grabbed Jim's arm and pulled him from the smoldering campfire, his blood sizzling as it dripped into the flames. And then, by the light of the headlights, the men set up a tripod while, working gingerly, Johnson lifted a long tube from the trunk.

6

A solid, dimensional overhead view of the B-3 was moving across the computer screen, over a map of west-central Colorado. The map moved with minute-hand slowness as the bomber flew west, with Missouri and Kansas and most of Colorado behind it.

"Climb to nineteen thousand on heading two-eight-seven," Hale said.

"Copy," Deakins replied. "One-nine on two-eighty-seven. What'd you hear about your slot in the Aurora Project?"

"Doesn't look like it's gonna happen," Hale told him.

"Did you talk to Taylor like I said?"

Hale nodded.

"And?"

"He told me I haven't got enough fighter hours to get into the pool."

"Really?" Deakins said. "And did you tell him you can outfly some of those winged peckers with *half* your time?"

"I said, 'Thank you, sir. Good-bye.'" Hale shot Deakins a look. "And don't say it."

"Don't say what?" Deakins asked. "That you just caved in?"

"Yeah," Hale said, "don't say that. I mean, what was I gonna do, lie?"

"No," Deakins said. "Sell yourself."

"That's just another word for fight," Hale said.

"So? What's wrong with that?"

"What's wrong is that—Christ," said Hale, exasperated. "Don't you get it? If all you've got is a hammer, how long before everything starts looking like a nail?"

"That's deep," Deakins said. "Fact is, I'd rather be the hammer than the nail. I'd rather act than react."

"Good. And would you rather be a major than a colonel?" Hale asked.

Deakins fired him a look. "Touché," he said. "You nailed me good with that one."

"Sorry," Hale continued, "but you would've been, you know. If only you knew when to back off. Or at least *who* to back off from."

"Maybe you shoulda written me a list, copilot. A promotion crib sheet."

Hale shook his head. "You could've figured all that out. But like I've been telling you for years, we're different."

"I know," Deakins said. "You say tomato, I say to*mah*to . . ."

Hale smirked. "I get the feeling that's something else before my time."

Deakins grinned. "Yeah," he said. He adjusted the helmet microphone, which was the size of a fresh pencil eraser, and clicked on. "Uh . . . Ghost Seven to McMurran. Hey, Wilkins, you ground-pounding bag of shit. Your boys in Utah still awake?"

The voice of Colonel Max Wilkins came back smartly. "Copy, Mr. Deakins. We're ready and waiting. Be advised we're gonna snatch your sorry little asses this evening and bite down hard. You may pass that along to Mr. Hale with my compliments."

Deakins shut off the microphone and looked across the cockpit at Hale. "Willy Boy is giving us 'tude. You want to take it through tonight?"

"Absotively," said Hale. "Tell the good colonel I'll fly this puppy right through his knees and mail his dick back to him."

Deakins smiled. He flicked the microphone back on. "Copy, Colonel. Captain Hale says if anyone can catch us, it'll be you."

"Copy," said Wilkins. "I'm sure that's what he said. More likely it was, 'Tell the colonel I can fly this through his spreading ass cheeks without him knowing.'"

Deakins swallowed a laugh. "No, Colonel. I assure you, he did not say that."

"Yeah, right. Tell me another one, Mother Goose."

Deakins grinned as he reached forward and pushed a blue button on the console. He heard a click in the built-in headphones. "Command, this is Ghost Seven. Approaching enemy radar. Switching to mission mode."

"We copy," said a voice.

Deakins glanced at the digital readout beneath one of the monitors. They seemed brighter, now that the world outside was dark. "Mark oh-one-two-nine. Over."

"Roger that mark, Ghost Seven. See you on the other side. Over and out."

Deakins pushed a red button beside the blue one, which sent the radio back to the AWACS. He said nothing, just listened as the Kid put his crew through their doomed-to-fail paces.

"Everyone get a fix," Wilkins said evenly. "They're about to turn off the lights."

Poor Willy Boy, Deakins thought. *Always chasing rainbows and ghosts, and never catching any of them. He's not ahead of the curve, like us.*

Well, he thought, *not like me.*

Deakins glanced at Hale. "Ready, Captain?"

Hale was looking at the topographic display. His right hand was on the control stick, his left hovered over a horizontal panel with three buttons: Take Off, Mission, and Landing.

"On your command," Hale said.

Deakins checked the airspeed and height. "Twenty-five thousand feet, four hundred MPH. Dead on, Captain. Go to war."

Hale pressed the Mission button and the B-3 went into full Stealth mode: outside running lights off, noise dampeners engaged, contrail gone, and control panel dark save for the eight screens, which went from bright to dim.

Though the microphone had gone off, the radio receiver was still hot and Deakins stayed tuned to the conversation in the AWACS.

"Lost 'em on IFF," Wilkins said moments after the Mission button was pressed. "Who's still got 'em?"

A voice at Wilkins's side trumpeted, "I've got their heat signature, sir."

Deakins listened closely.

"Their engines may be cold," the voice continued, "but the background's colder. The B-3 is smack over Grand Junction."

So the fuzzheads have us, Deakins thought. *For the moment.* In his mind's eye, he could see the screen in the AWACS—the background, a waveform pattern, with the sharp triangle of the B-3 moving across it.

The major looked at the map of the targets on the computer screen, center-top. The "hostile" radar sites, the bogus targets in Utah, were blinking red. His eyes moved backward along the Colorado River, which wriggled like a polygraph line between the two states.

"Hale," Deakins said, "descend to four hundred feet AGL. River valley approach. Go to point-seven mach."

"Airspeed point-seven mach," Hale repeatedly calmly. "That's point-one over maximum."

"She can handle it," Deakins said. "At least, that's what the computers tell us. Time to find out if they're right."

Hale said, "Airspeed lock at point-seven mach. Blue line descent on throttle to four hundred feet AGL." He began pulling back on the throttle. "Time to limbo down, see if we can surprise them with how low we can go."

"Oh, they'll be surprised," Deakins said with a grin. "I promise you that."

7

Terry Carmichael liked working the graveyard shift.

The park was quiet enough this time of year, but at night it was positively dead. Quiet enough so that she could listen to her Japanese language tapes on the cassette player in her truck. Quiet enough to enjoy the kind of serenity few humans had experienced since the dawn of the industrial age. Quiet enough so that she could think, objectively, about the string of hardcore losers she'd managed to fall for with increasing regularity during the last ten of her twenty-eight years.

There was the love of her life, Eddie, who sat next to her in the Romantic English Novel class in college and ran off to London to write a romantic English novel. He wrote to her years later to say he was managing a medical supply warehouse in Miami and could he please come visit her?

There was Ari, her martial arts *sensei*, who was teaching her how to fall after hours and convinced her to stay on the mat. Later, she learned that he was giving horizontal instructions to every young lady in the dojo.

More recently there was her neighbor Joe, who got married and moved; Louis, whom she met at the movies on a particularly lonely Friday and who turned out to be schizophrenic; and Mick, the Parks Department official and professional asshole who was going to leave his wife "soon" and never did.

"*Arigato,*" she repeated after Yuki said it on the tape. "Thank you."

It wasn't her fault, she told herself. It very clearly was not.

"*Sumimasen,*" she said after Yuki. "Pardon me."

It was men . . . all of them

"*Kudsai,*" she said after Yuki. "Please."

They courted you till they had you, and then it was on to the next trophy. Or they held onto you until they got what they needed, then gave you the heave-ho. What was it about men that made them so superficial?

"*Ottoh,*" she repeated. "Husband."

And desirable? she thought bitterly. Why did she come back to them each time she swore off them?

Her radio bleeped. Terry ejected the tape, grabbed the microphone, and tapped the Talk switch with her thumb.

"Yes, Clyde?" she said.

"Terry, have you been through the Needles entrance tonight?"

"*Ee-eh,*" she said.

"Come again?"

"That was 'no' in Japanese. Why do you ask?"

"Mrs. Parker called," Clyde said.

Terry rolled her big blue eyes. "Oh, God. What is it this time—UFO abduction or ritual human sacrifice?"

"Neither. She said she saw a bunch of trucks going through the Needles entrance an hour ago, and thought they looked suspicious."

"Clyde, what's a suspicious truck look like?" she asked. "Was there a mask on the window? Were werewolves driving?"

"C'mon, Terry—"

"Sorry, Clyde," she said, "but this is a woman who chopped

34

off one of her own fingers because she said it 'turned' on her. It was one of the evil dead."

"Yeah, she's a nutburger," Clyde agreed. "Thing is, she said one of the trucks was ours and described it right. I've got to have it checked, and you're the only one out."

Terry sighed. "Maybe Bigfoot got a driver's license."

"Terry—"

"Yeah, yeah," she said. "Don't worry. I'll look into it. But, Clyde?"

"What?"

"If she comes at me with a stake and hammer, like the time she thought I was Dracula's niece, you're dead meat."

"Hey," said Clyde, "you're the one who said you wanted the graveyard shift this month."

Terry said, "That was only so you'd stop asking me out. I'll get over there and let you know what I find."

Returning the microphone to its hook, Terry sighed more deeply than before, pushed the tape back in, and swung the truck around.

"*Hai*," she said after Yuki. "Yes. *Shimbun*. Newspaper. *Hoteru*. Hotel. *Parker-san*. Pain in the butt. . . ."

Deakins listened with satisfaction as Wilkins's crewman reported that he'd lost the B-3.

"Keep hunting," Wilkins said, less gung-ho than before. "They're gonna have to come up for air sooner or later." The colonel was silent for a moment, then said, "Deak, if you're listening—I don't know what you just pulled out there, but you will be mine. Oh, yes."

Deakins smiled. *Oh no I won't*, he thought as he looked at the radar data on one of the screens. "Okay, Hale. We're under their eyes and ears. Proceed to primary target."

Hale nodded. "Descending to two hundred."

Deakins's eyes were on the topographic screen. "Ridge coming up in six seconds."

"Got it," said Hale. His left hand moved above a yellow button. "You know, these exercises are fantastic. I mean, when that day finally comes and we go to war against Utah—man, we're really going to kick ass."

Deakins continued to watch the topographic display as Hale pushed the button to engage the autopilot. An almost imperceptible steadying occurred throughout the aircraft, reminiscent of a car going over to cruise control.

Hale released the stick and glanced out the forward windscreen. The stars were bright, the moon sharp-edged.

"Nicely done," said Deakins. "You're getting to be as good as me." He looked at Hale. "You really love this shit, don't you?"

Hale took a deep breath. "Like you love boxing. Remember when we were out on the lake last week and you asked me why I became a pilot?"

"All I remember is eating the big, juicy bass I caught while you sucked on the bones of the poor scrawny little thing you hauled in."

Hale's eyes had a dreamy softness. It was as if he hadn't heard Deakins's response. "I said I became an Air Force pilot because where else can you fly a two-billion-dollar plane eight hundred miles an hour? Do it so low to the ground that you can reach down and goose the ladies? And that's true. But it's also for this."

Hale extended both hands toward the window, as though they held an offering.

"I mean," Hale said, "when we're up here, I feel . . . well, closer somehow." His hands dropped to his knees. "Shit, I don't know how to put it. I'm not even sure exactly what it is I'm trying to say."

Deakins said, "You feel closer to God? Is that what it is?"

"Maybe. I mean, that doesn't make any sense, does it, since God is supposed to be everywhere. What should it matter if you're in the clouds at mach-something or lying in a grass hut in Sumatra?"

"It shouldn't matter," Deakins agreed.

"So why do I feel like this is a kind of religious experience?"

"Because it is, my friend."

Hale looked at him, interested. "You being serious?"

"Yeah," Deakins went on. "With the payload we're carrying, we *are* God."

Hale's interest became dismay. "What the hell are you talking about?"

"The Old Testament," Deakins said. "Noah's flood, Sodom and Gomorrah, the Golden Calf. We're the God who smiteth."

Hale shook his head. "Jesus, Deak. I was thinking of something a little more . . . pious."

"Oooo . . . we can't have any of that naughty fighting, right, pard?"

Hale's mood soured even more. "Jesus, Deak, don't get back on that kick—"

"Why not? You don't find what you're saying even a little hypocritical?"

"What?"

"That you come on like this big pacifist," Deakins said, "but you get your jollies being part of a fighting force."

"The U.S. military doesn't have a chip on its shoulder," Hale said. "They want peace. I want peace. We were made for each other."

"A marriage made in Heaven," Deak said. "Obviously, by God himself."

"Yeah," Hale said. "I like to think so."

"Which means you're in this for the long haul," Deakins said. "Till death do you part."

"Abso-fucking-lutely," Hale said. "Don't tell me you aren't."

"I don't know."

"A guy with your natural ability—"

"To offend people?" Deakins suggested. "You said so yourself."

"No," Hale said, "I mean to fly. You know your body, man, I feel that in the ring. When you're in here, your body becomes part of the plane—you *are* the machine."

"Nice of you to notice," Deakins said. "But I'm coming up on twenty years and I'm thinking that maybe you're right.

Maybe I never had the right attitude for this company. Like you said, I should be a colonel by now."

"Hey, Deak—we were just shootin' the shit, that's all. Anyway, don't talk like it's too late. It isn't. You give a little, they'll give a little."

"No," Deakins said, "I'll never be a colonel. Shitlumps like Boone make general."

"Boone's okay," said Hale.

"C'mon. A thought goes through his head, it's been on the shortest trip in North America." Deakins looked out the windscreen. "Twenty years of watching idiots climb past you takes its toll. Fact is, I'm thinking about cashing out."

"No way," Hale said emphatically. "You'd miss it before you even left."

"I don't know about that," Deakins said. "Flying doesn't mean as much to me as it does to you."

"Not flying," Hale said. "Carrying nukes. To me they're just cargo. But you get off having that power. You just said it your—"

"Hold it!" Deakins barked. He held up an index finger as he looked down at his screen. He looked out the window and frowned.

"What is it?" Hale asked.

"Take a look out your side. I think our terrain following is off. Shouldn't starboard ridge be on our port?"

Hale was all business now. He looked. "It seems okay to me," he said.

While Hale looked, Deakins slipped off his right-hand glove and reached into his flight suit.

Hale turned back. His gaze went from Deakins's narrowed eyes to a thin cylinder he was pulling from his suit.

"Jesus, Deak, you can't smoke in—"

Hale bit off the rest of the sentence as Deakins pointed the cylinder at Hale's forehead. It wasn't a cigarette but the slender barrel of a Walther P38.

"Don't budge," Deakins said flatly.

"What do you mean?" Hale said.

Deakins said quietly, almost sadly, "I've decided, actually, to cash out now."

"Deak, you can't mean this. Come on, man. What the hell kind of joke is this?"

"No joke," Deakins said. "I'm sorry, partner."

As Deakins's finger closed on the trigger, Hale threw his right arm forward. He caught the outside of Deakins's wrist, driving the major's forearm across his face as the gun discharged. The bullet drilled a clean path through the crown of Hale's helmet and punched through the window, leaving a whistling hole and a weblike design in its wake. Deakins's finger was still on the trigger and the gun continued to fire, smashing holes in the ceiling and wall of the cockpit.

"*Deak*, it's me!" Hale screamed. "What's going *on?*"

Deakins didn't answer. He stopped firing, brought his left hand around, and fought to aim the gun back at Hale.

Greater strength and deeper desire enabled Deakins to swing the barrel toward Hale. He squeezed off another round, which ripped through the top of Hale's belt harness, causing the shoulder strap to snap. The bullet hit a buckle and bounced off.

Free of his harness, Hale suddenly yelled and threw his body weight into his arms, slamming the gun hard against the front of Deakins's helmet.

The major yowled. But despite the ringing pain in his forehead he kept his grip on the gun and his eyes on the captain. Then, beyond Hale, Deakins saw the dark sky grow darker, the stars disappear from the bottom up.

They were banking toward a cliff.

Deakins roared inarticulately, then wrested his gunhand free and grabbed the control stick with his left hand. He yanked hard to the right, swinging the bomber away from the cliff and into a sweeping right turn.

The rapid turn threw Hale across the throttle and against Deakins. His back against the side of the cockpit, Deakins was able to throw Hale off.

And then Deakins saw it. The brilliant red laser light shot through the sky like blood from a paper cut, fine and straight. Deakins took advantage of Hale's momentary imbalance to pull off his left-hand glove with his teeth and use his index and middle finger to push the armaments control buttons One, Two, Right.

When he pushed the buttons, Deakins automatically activated a computer program that gave the pilot a graphic indication of what was happening in the bomb bay. The cartoonlike animation showed the bomb racks rotating. The picture stopped moving when the two B-83s, glowing red, were locked in the bottom spot, the release position.

"You *bastard*!" Hale screamed, and dove for him again.

Deakins brought the gun around, though not before Hale was on top of him. Deakins tried to angle the gun at his adversary's back, but his own tight harness made that impossible.

"You're friggin' crazy!" Hale snarled in his face as he grabbed the sides of Deakins's helmet.

With his free hand, Deakins tried to stop him. Hale yanked the helmet off and slammed it hard into his opponent's face.

"You're *crazy*, you *hear* me?"

Deakins did, but didn't care what Hale thought or said. Momentarily dazed, he'd lost the gun. As he felt for it in the dark, he found the plane's compact fire extinguisher instead. It came free with a tug.

Roaring again, Deakins smashed the metal cylinder into Hale's cheekbone and nose. Blood exploded from the captain's left nostril and he fell back, groggy, as the plane flew closer to the laser beam.

Deakins struggled to fight down his rage. ETA was in less than half a minute; there was no more time for this, and no time to find the gun. There was only one thing to do—not foolproof by a long shot, but with the busted shoulder strap it was a damn good bet.

Reaching across the throttle, Deakins clicked the ejection control button on Hale's seat from Auto to Manual. Then he slid his hand beside the seat and wrapped his fingers around the soft rubber of the ejection handle.

"Sorry, pal," Deakins said, licking blood from his lip where the helmet had struck it.

His eyes half-shut, Hale made a vain, valiant lunge for the handle as Deakins pulled it.

There was a loud pop, a hiss, and the ejection hatch blew open. At the same time, Hale's head snapped back hard and acrid smoke billowed through the cockpit like flattened cotton balls as the seat rose through the opening, carrying Hale with it.

As the red laser beam slashed through the windows, tinting the smoke ruby as it was sucked out the opening, Deakins batted away wind-whipped printouts and coffee cups and reached for the button marked Release.

The fist of cold air slammed down on Hale, reviving him and at the same time making it difficult for him to breathe. The B-3 was already hundreds of feet above and beyond him and vanishing rapidly.

The chair was rocking wildly from side to side—or was it him? Hale wondered. He had been through countless ejection drills, and even as the parachute splashed open above him, he knew at once that something was wrong.

The shoulder harness. He remembered it had snapped. All that was holding him to the seat was the waist buckle, which he never wore tight because it made him want to pee.

An instant before the parachute was fully deployed, Hale flung his arms across his chest, felt desperately in the dark for the remnants of the harness, and wrapped his freezing fingers around them before the chute jerked his seat violently. The seat belt dug hard into his waist as he was thrown up against it, but he held on as the chair slowed, descending almost lazily now, with gentle, pendulumlike swings.

The air was cold on his bloody face, and the sweat under his flight suit cooled, then chilled rapidly. But Hale wasn't thinking about his discomfort or about what the major might have in mind. All he could think about was that his friend—or someone who he'd *believed* was his friend—had betrayed him. In rapid succession, Deak had tried to put a hole in his forehead and boot him out the door of a speeding bomber. As difficult as it was to remain conscious, it was tougher to forget what had just happened and let himself pass out.

Hale compromised by allowing himself to sob briefly from the shock, after which he blinked away his tears and looked down, trying to make out, in the dark, the shape of any trees or rivers he might be in danger of hitting. . . .

9

Terry Carmichael stood beside the open driver's side window of her truck. One hand was on the cocked hip of her snug green trousers; the other held her radio.

She hit the Talk button. "Clyde?"

"I'm here, light of my life."

"You can tell Mrs. Parker that there's nothing weird going on here. No truck, no UFOs. And except for the odd human head on a stake, no sign of Satan."

"Would you care to tell her yourself?" Clyde asked. "I can patch you through—"

"No, thanks," she said.

"It'll just take a second, Terry. She's probably waiting right beside the phone."

"Clyde, isn't it about time for your medication . . ."

Terry looked up, the last word trailing off as she felt the air move. It wasn't the wind. It was more like the body-shaking vibration of a jackhammer going full-tilt. Only the vibrations rattled every inch of her, from scalp to heel.

"Terry?" Clyde asked. "Are you okay?"

"Shhhh," she said, though not into the microphone, or loud enough for him to hear.

"Terry?"

"Quiet!" she barked, her eyebrows pinching in the center as the rumbling rose and she trembled all over, as though she were standing on a drum. She glanced to the right, saw her truck quaking.

Then she heard it, felt it, and saw it all at once. She heard the ocean-roar rush of air; felt it whip her long brown hair around, turn up the collar of her green shirt, and cause her pant legs to flutter about her shins; saw it pass overhead, dark and wide and fast. Terry ducked reflexively, even through the blotch was past her before she did, and she knew that it—whatever "it" was, because it sure didn't sound like a plane—couldn't possibly be *that* low.

"Holy shit," she muttered as the afterwash died quickly and the skyborne shadow was swallowed up somewhere to the west, among the stars and trees.

And as she looked at where the maelstrom had last been—could it have been a freak kind of tornado?—she saw another shape, less *Night on Bald Mountain*ish, floating earthward roughly a quarter mile away.

"Tehhh-ry!" Clyde sang out.

She clicked on. "Yeah, I'm here."

"Would you mind telling me what's going on?"

"I don't know," she said. "I saw something fall. I'm going to check. And Clyde?"

"Yes?"

"If Mrs. Parker calls to say she saw a UFO, tell her I know all about it."

Signing off before her supervisor could waste her time with questions she couldn't answer, Terry reached into the truck to replace the microphone, snatched the flashlight from the dashboard, and set out through the hip-high brush.

10

When he released the bombs, Deakins used the heel of his right hand to push out the remains of the shattered window, poked his forehead out, and watched the warheads fall. They tumbled to earth gracefully, like branches spinning in a fast-moving river. They were harmless in their current mode; they would only be dangerous when they were activated.

The B-3 was too far away for Deakins to see them, even before the bombs were gobbled up by the treetops. Settling back in his seat and drawing air through his clenched teeth, he took a moment to collect himself. Then he picked up his helmet, put it on gingerly—Hale had hurt him with the whack in the face—and pushed the Landing button on the mission mode panel.

The cockpit lit up.

"I got 'em!" a voice in Wilkins's command said.

Deakins heard Wilkins say, "But they're not due to come out of Stealth for another half hour. Something must be—"

"This is Deakins!" the major cut in, his tone frantic, grin wicked. "Hale lost it!"

"What do you mean?" Wilkins demanded. "Talk to me, Major. What is it?"

"Shit! Damn! I'm punching out!"

Still smiling, Deakins reprogrammed the autopilot to head for the sandy flats four miles west, quickly inputting in the coordinates and rate of descent. Then he turned the autopilot on, switched the Ejection button to Manual, made sure his harness was snug—experiencing a moment of sorrow for poor, unbridled Hale, who probably landed with a splat a mile from his seat—and pulled the handle. The hatch flew off with a *blam* and a *whoosh*, and a moment later Deakins was blasted free of the bomber.

First there were two seconds of crushing G-force as his seat rocketed up and away from the plane. Then there was the moment of weightlessness as he reached the zenith of the ejection arc and began to drop. And finally there was the chest-abrading tug as the parachute deployed and slowed his descent. A moment later he was floating to earth like a soap bubble.

The B-3, however, was not.

As planned, it continued to the west, descending three feet a second. From his lofty post, Deakins could see the black flying wing slice lower, gently lower, moment by moment, until it bellied down, skidding and pinwheeling gently to the left, in the open expanse of sand. The granules rose in cloudy waves around the nose and right wing of the B-3 as it scudded to a stop. Then, lit by the still-glowing light of the cockpit, the grains of sand snowed down on the plane like glitter.

Looking down as he approached a clear spot on an escarpment, Deakins savored the thought of all the "What the hells" and "Jesus Christs" which would be exploding from the mouths of the crew in the AWACS and the folks at Whiteman and at McMurran AFB here in Utah.

He savored even more the fact that the rubes would never know what hit them.

Not until it was too late, anyway.

11

Lieutenant Colonel Sam Rhodes was a priest.

At least, that's what his men called him behind his back. Father Rhodes. They joked that the pinnacle of his career would not be making general but Pope.

The trim, fifty-four-year-old officer didn't drink, he never swore, and he had the Bible, Old Testament and New, loaded on the hard drive of his laptop. He believed in killing, but only if an adversary struck first. That didn't mean they had to kill first: just attack. The Bible went along with him on that: the commandment, historically mistranslated, did not forbid killing, only murder. And it wasn't murder to kill an oppressor. It was justice.

As he stood on the floodlit tarmac at McMurran Air Force Base, his gray buzzcut bristling in the rotor wash of the Black Hawk helicopter, Rhodes had to fight to keep from swearing as he waved on the four men who were running toward him.

A B-3 possibly down, with two nuclear missiles onboard and the potential for deadly, widespread radioactive contamination. This was what he had feared when he first heard of the plan—and it was *exactly* the kind of Armageddon scenario the

Bible talked about in Revelation 16:17: "And the seventh angel poured out his vial into the air. . . ."

When the men arrived, he urged them on with a look. They clambered into the combat assault chopper, which was equipped with a cargo hook with an external-lift capacity of eight thousand pounds. If the plane *had* gone down, and it was safe enough to get close, Rhodes hoped that they'd be able to recover the bombs at least and bring them back.

As Rhodes was about to get onboard, two beeps of a horn stopped him. He looked behind him as a jeep pulled up and Colonel Wilkins climbed from the passenger's side.

"Sam!" the stockier, older, balding officer yelled to be heard over the rotor.

The men exchanged salutes.

"Yes, Max?" asked Rhodes.

He said loudly, "I just wanted to tell you, face-to-face, not to do anything reckless."

"Such as?"

Wilkins made a face. "You know exactly what I'm talking about. If those nukes are hot, I don't want you sticking around as penance."

Rhodes nodded once.

Wilkins's beefy face grew stern. "I mean it, Sam. I know this is your home state and you were opposed to the drill to begin with. But if there's a problem, let the experts handle it. Do I have your word on that?"

"You do," Rhodes said. "But I'll tell you this: somebody really blew it, and we're going to find out who, how, and why."

"No argument there," Wilkins said. "And when we do, it'll be an eye for an eye. I promise."

With a grateful smile and another salute, Rhodes climbed into the hatch. Seconds later, the powerful General Electric turboshafts whining, the black chopper rose quickly and disappeared into the night.

12

White House Chief of Staff Mason Baird rubbed his three A.M. shadow as he entered the Situation Room at the Pentagon.

"So," he said, "now that *we're* all up and jump-started with caffeine, do I wake the President?"

His assistant, Giles Prentice, followed him in, his baby face red from a quick, latherless shaving.

Baird's question was greeted by a long silence from the other men and women in the brightly lit chamber. Chairman of the Joint Chiefs of Staff Jeff Dryfoos stared at his tightly folded hands. Air Force General Nick Creeley looked down into his black coffee. Their collective team of fourteen assistants and deputies, in uniforms or suits, looked at one another across the long, black conference table, or at telephones, fax machines, computer monitors, keyboards, and the backlit maps on the walls.

Finally, Dryfoos spoke. "Where is the President?"

"In Las Vegas," Baird said as he took the only free seat. Giles stood behind him. "Computer convention. Some warmed-over information superhighway crap."

Baird scooted the chair noisily, then lifted his wire-rimmed glasses and rubbed his eyes. The remnants of sleep didn't want to leave and he thought back bitterly to nearly thirty years ago, when he was a gung-ho first selectman in a small town in Connecticut. Late-night meetings were a cinch then, and he used to use them to wrest concessions from the tired, older second selectmen. Now that he was a tired, older White House chief of staff, who had been torn from bed by a knock at the door just thirty-seven minutes before, he had a desire to go back and smack his cocky, younger self—not to mention Major Harry Hall, the officer who had been sent to fetch him and Giles hither.

Of course, it was ironic that he had had loads of energy back when he had to worry about things like the budget for the little red schoolhouse and the volunteer fire department, not a missing B-3 and a pair of nuclear bombs.

The chairman filled his barrel chest and said, "You don't have to wake him, Mase, but let's make sure his staff knows. We don't want him to hit the remote in the morning and hear about it from Bryant Gumbel."

Baird nodded. "Sounds like a plan. What else?"

The chairman pointed to the computer monitor to Baird's right. He tapped the keys on his own PC and a document appeared on Baird's screen.

"We're going out with this," Dryfoos said. "Ric's team prepared it."

Baird stole a quick look at portly, bearded Richard Meyers. He could tell, from the Pentagon press liaison officer's cherubic smile, that he had gone for the sweet lie.

Baird mumbled as he read, " 'United States Air Force regrets to announce . . . a C-130 heavy-lift cargo plane went down over the Utah desert . . . status of the crew has not been determined at this time . . .' yadda, yadda, yadda." He looked at Meyers. "Nice bullshit, Ric."

"Thank you," said Meyers.

Baird heard Giles's new shoes squeak as he shifted behind him.

"No. Wait. We're making a mistake," the thirty-year-old said.

Baird half-turned. His look said, *Why are you contradicting me, Bernie?* He asked flatly, "Why do you think that, Bernie?"

Giles either failed to catch the look or, more likely, didn't care. The kid had strong opinions.

"*Aviation Week* has been following the B-3 for years," Giles said. "They've got stringers who take their vacations in Knob Noster, Missouri, so they can sit in a lawn chair all night long by the Whiteman perimeter fence just in case a B-3 takes off. Sirs, the boys in those lawn chairs know a B-3 took off tonight. They're going to know when it doesn't come back. And when we put out a press release saying that a C-130 went down in Utah, they're going to run a story about what really happened. Then everyone'll know the truth, and we're going to look really stupid."

"Thank you, Giles," Baird said. "You have a good point." He looked at Dryfoos. "But there's something else to consider, and that is do we really need this?"

"I agree," said General Mike Schneider, newly returned from the DMZ between North and South Korea. "Who the hell reads *Aviation Week* anyway?"

"For starters," said Giles, "the military reporters at *Time, Newsweek, The Washington Post*—"

"Okay." Baird held up a hand. "Another good point. But we can deny this stronger than a guy in a lawn chair can prove it."

"We sure can," Meyers agreed.

Baird said, "Think of what'll happen if the truth comes out in a time of budgetary austerity. That a secret, twenty-seven-billion-dollar new-plane program has been going on—and that roughly one ninth of that money might be a pile of useless crap somewhere in Utah."

General Schneider added, "And then the President and the Pentagon will have the environmentalists up their butts because the bomber might have gone down in a national park with a couple of nuclear warheads that could be leaking."

"Yeah, why should anyone worry about something like that?" Dryfoos asked. He looked at Giles. "What do you suggest?"

Giles shrugged. "These are all valid points, but if it were up to me I'd just say a B-3 went down. Report that it was FOD'ed."

Air Force General Nick Creeley sighed. "Foreign object damaged. Northrop's gonna love that."

"They'll live," said Dryfoos.

Schneider shook his head. "What are you going to tell the press, that a bird flew into the engine? Isn't that rather unlikely with the B-3, Nick?"

Creeley said, "It's unlikely, but plausible. And for the record, I agree with Giles. A simple dose of the truth will earn us a respectful period of grace from *AW*. But a lie will turn them into pit bulls."

Baird exhaled loudly. He gave Ric an apologetic look. "Rewrite it," he said.

Ric continued to smile, though now it fell short of his eyes. "And say what?"

"Exactly what Giles just said."

"Yes, sir," Ric said glumly.

Baird half-turned back to Giles again. "You got a toothbrush?"

"Sir?"

"I want you in Utah as soon as possible," Baird said. "I want to know everything that's going on. I want you to make sure that the plane went nowhere near the Uintah and Ouray Indian Reservation, and that no one there is upset. I want to know if an owl shits funny from possible radiation."

53

"You want to know everything," Giles repeated.

"Right. And one thing more," Baird's gaze shifted to Dryfoos. "If this turns out to be sabotage, we don't go to trial. We go to General Quirk at the CIA and General Roger Michaels at the National Crisis Management Center. This baby's the next generation of our national defense, and the person or persons responsible *will* be maximally demoted."

Dryfoos and Creeley didn't say a word, but Schneider gave Baird an enthusiastic thumbs-up.

13

The Black Hawk swept in low over the treetops, its side-mounted searchlights startling deer and getting annoyed looks from foxes, its rotors spinning up sand as it entered the flatlands.

Lieutenant Colonel Rhodes was standing behind the pilot, Clint McKellar, as they flew over the park at a cruising speed of 150 miles an hour. There was no need to go slowly: it wasn't as if the B-3 would be easy to miss.

And he didn't miss it.

Off to the northeast, the spotlight played across the black wing of the plane jutting at an ugly angle from the sand.

"Hold it," Rhodes said. "Come back."

"I saw it," said McKellar.

The pilot pushed the control stick gently toward the wreckage, at the same time spiraling down. The props blew the golden sand from the fuselage: Rhodes's heart swelled when he saw that the hatches had been blown. Which meant that at least the pilots had gotten free of the aircraft and were probably all right.

He turned to Lieutenants Bill Kelly, Don Reed, and Pat Thomas, who were sitting in the spacious cabin.

"We've found it," he said. "Anything, Pat?"

Young Pat Thomas looked at the Geiger counter resting beside him on the bench. He nodded about as slow as he chewed his gum. "No, sir. Only a faint background glow from the old mines. Otherwise, no radiation."

Rhodes offered a silent prayer of thanksgiving, then radioed Colonel Wilkins from the cockpit with the news.

"Great," Wilkins said. "A lot of people here are going to breathe easier when I tell them that."

Less than two minutes later, the helicopter had settled into the sands fewer than a hundred yards from the B-3. The four officers had donned helmets with windshields to protect them from the spinning sands, and were approaching the plane single-file, at a jog. Rhodes was in the lead, his flashlight picking out areas the chopper spotlights missed.

"Colonel Wilkins, do you copy?" Rhodes yelled into his helmet microphone.

"I copy," Wilkins replied. "What's it look like?"

"Well, she didn't come apart in flight, that's for sure," he said. "Crashed whole. Can't see one wing—the other's bent up, maybe even severed . . . can't tell from here."

Rhodes motioned the other men toward the bomb bay while he went to the cockpit. He shined his light from one side to the other.

"Wilkins? Cockpit's empty," he reported, "and the seats are gone. My men are checking the payload now. I'm going to join them."

"Copy that," Wilkins said.

Rhodes had to fight from being blown sideways as he walked along the dented side of the aircraft. *It is strange,* he thought, *how in death a person seems so pathetically frail, while a plane like this retains traces of its dignity.*

Maybe because the ultimate strength of humans is in the soul, he thought, *and not in their lines or carriage.*

56

The big, smooth fuselage was tilted slightly to one side, like a beached blue whale. The right bomb bay door was exposed and the men had been pulling it open by hand. They had opened it nearly a foot when Rhodes arrived.

"We'll have it in another minute or so," Reed called back to him.

Rhodes shouted, "No! That's enough!" It wasn't important that they actually get inside: he just wanted to make absolutely sure that the bombs were secure.

The men stepped back as Rhodes walked over. Dropping to his knees under the fuselage and leaning to the right, Rhodes shined the flashlight inside.

His eyes widened as the beam roamed back to front along the empty racks. Not believing what he didn't see, Rhodes pulled off his helmet and squirmed the top half of his torso and one arm inside. Thinking that maybe the bombs had been shaken loose, he shined the light around the bomb bay.

They hadn't been knocked free. They were gone.

Rhodes ducked out and pulled his helmet back on. "Colonel?" he shouted into the microphone.

"I'm here, Sam."

"Forget about breathing easier," Rhodes said. "I'm afraid we've got ourselves a broken arrow."

14

Still sitting in the Situation Room, with fewer people but more empty coffee cups, Mason Baird looked at Joint Chiefs Chairman Dryfoos. Like Schneider, Creeley, and six aides, the men were wearing headphones plugged into jacks underneath the conference table.

They had been listening to the communication between Lieutenant Colonel Rhodes and McMurran.

Baird doffed his headset. "Broken arrow?" he asked Dryfoos.

The chairman said matter-of-factly, "That's what we call it when we lose a nuclear weapon."

"Oh, Jesus," Baird said. He rolled his lips together and shook his head. "I don't know what's scarier. Losing nuclear weapons or the fact that it happens so often you people have a term for it."

Schneider said, "The terms were created for war simulations. This only happened once before. Remember the Greek cruise ship which went down in August 1991?"

"Can't say I do," Baird said. "Or maybe I'm just blanking because I'm in a state of shock."

"Well, the SEALS did that. The ship was transporting a

stolen nuke to South Africa. Hell, that's why the crew abandoned ship before the passengers did—caught hell for it later, too. Didn't want to get their stones fried." He chuckled. "That's why the South African Air Force rescued so many of the people. They wanted to get them the hell out of there so they could try to salvage the goddamned nuke."

Baird shuddered—now because of the way that had amused Schneider. These guys played too *many* war games, he decided. To them, it was all a big *Dr. Strangelove* role-playing game.

"What do you think?" Dryfoos asked Creeley. "Software malfunction and accidental discharge?"

"It's certainly possible," General Creeley replied. "Improper debugging . . . or it could be a radiation leak that affected the—"

Wilkins's voice in the earphones cut the conversation short.

"Sam, Colonel Marrow and I agree that you should go look for the nukes. But keep the counter near you. If those eggs hit rock, they could've cracked."

"Understood."

"Your Geigers pick up more rads than you'd get off a toaster oven," Wilkins warned, "I want you out of there. I'm ordering in gunships for support—just in case anything funny's going on."

"I copy," Rhodes said. "We'll take off and start back along the flight path—I'll be in touch."

"Remember what I said, Sam."

"I will, Colonel," Rhodes replied.

Baird shook his head again as he thought back to the last thing Dryfoos and Creeley had been saying.

"Let me get this straight," the White House chief of staff said. "Two nuclear bombs dropped from a plane, but they didn't go off. Does that mean our bombs don't work either?"

"What do you mean 'either'?" Schneider said, sitting up in his chair.

"Well, the plane—"

"We don't know why the B-3 went down," the general said. "In his last transmission, Major Deakins said that Captain Hale lost control of the aircraft. It's possible one of them activated the weapons release system in confusion."

"You *do* train these pilots, I trust?" Baird asked.

"They're the best in the world," General Creeley said indignantly. "But believe me, Mr. Baird. When you're in a ten-ton plane augering in at mach one, you start pushing every button in sight." Creeley rubbed the bridge of his nose. "Not that I want to pass judgment before we have the facts. For all we know, the B-3 *was* FOD'ed, in which case it's an act of God, not a screwup."

Dryfoos added, "And even if it wasn't a bird that knocked it down, the fact is as long as there are pilots, planes are going to crash."

Baird felt as if he'd been mugged—first by his own man, Giles, and now by the other side. He tried to remember what the hell it was that ever made him leave small town politics, anyway.

"To answer your question, Mr. Baird," said Creeley, his voice even, "this doesn't mean our bombs don't work. On the contrary, it means that they *do*. They're designed to survive crashes intact. They can lie in a pool of burning jet fuel for five hours without any problem."

Schneider folded his arms beneath a "take that" look—a last kick while Baird was down.

"It's only a matter of time before we find the warheads," Creeley continued. "When we do, you'll be impressed, I think, at how efficiently we implement our simulation scenarios."

Baird nodded, drained his coffee cup, and obviously disappointed Schneider by saying nothing. Privately, he hoped Creeley was correct: he'd be happy to eat crowburgers and *not* have to tell the President that a couple of nuclear bombs were missing.

But while he hoped it, twenty-plus years of acting on gut feelings that were usually correct told him not to heat up the skillet just yet.

15

Hale lay on his side, next to his ejection seat. His parachute was whipping in the wind, his head was throbbing inside his helmet, and he was slightly nauseated from the ride down.

Ejection was a lot rougher than in any of the simulations. Though now that he thought about it, fighting with Deakins and struggling to hold onto his shoulder harness probably had a lot to do with that. The ejectee was *supposed* to hold the shroud lines, not the harness, to try and control the landing somewhat. Instead, Hale had bounced off a tree and landed on his side before finally undoing his seat belt and spilling from the seat.

He pulled off his helmet and then lay there. He kept his eyes shut and didn't move, concentrating on the deep breathing exercises he'd been taught to marshal his strength. But his ears were still working—in spite of the pounding of whatever goddamn pulse was drumming up there—and after a few minutes he heard the gravelly crunch of footsteps approaching from behind. He continued to breathe deeply, listening as the footsteps stopped, and then he felt a hand on his shoulder.

Deakins, he surmised. He was nothing if not thorough, the son of a bitch.

Spinning around, fast and sure, Hale grabbed where the front of Deakins's flight suit would be and got a fistful of fabric. Then he rolled, pulling the figure with him, scrambled onto his knees, and straddled the newcomer. He cocked his left arm back, ready to jab the man as he'd never jabbed him in the ring.

And then he checked himself, because the man underneath him wasn't a man but a woman. A park ranger woman.

The woman didn't bother to check herself. Terry put the top of her thumb into the crook of her index finger, forming a hard pyramid with the thumb knuckle, and drove it into Hale's temple. The pain stretched from the top of his head to his shoulder, from earlobe to nose, and he went over like a bop bag, though he didn't spring up again.

Terry was on top of him, but she was at least sixty pounds lighter and wasn't there for long. Hale bucked up at the waist to distract her, then pushed her back. She fell on her shoulders, Hale slid from under her, and he was off like a sprinter at the gun.

Did park rangers have guns? he wondered, now that he thought of it. As he ran across the uneven, rocky terrain he dodged from side to side, head down, shoulders weaving. He was dizzy from the fall and from having gotten up too fast, and nearly stumbled as he ran.

Damn sliver of a moon, he thought as he cursed the darkness. Hale had never been the kind of man who looked up at the Milky Way in wonder and awe. Only machines and big buildings and other products of human industry impressed him. And right now, he would have traded all the stars and planets and that eggshell nothing of a moon for a good, heavy-with-D-cells flashlight.

"*Shit!*" Hale screamed, stopping short, arms pinwheeling like a cartoon character as he came suddenly to the edge of a cliff and a fifty-foot drop.

"That would be the wrong way," Terry said from behind him.

Hale spun around and saw the gun pointed in his direction; that answered *that* question. But he still had an option. There was a rock wall to the right, but in the other direction was a patch of trees about forty yards away. Beyond them, the cliff seemed to slope down gradually—

"You'd never make it down," Terry said. "Trust me."

"Why?" he asked.

"Why trust me?" she asked.

"No," he said. "Why would I never make it down?"

Terry said, "Because you'd have a bullet in each leg. Now raise 'em," she said, swinging the gun up as a visual aid.

Reluctantly, Hale did so. Terry waved him toward the rock wall. The cool stone felt good against his torn palms, though he resented the hell out of being ordered around.

"Hands behind you," she said.

"Look," Hale said, "I'm a captain in the United States Air Force—"

"Well, Captain," she said, "you're under arrest."

"Am I?" he said. "And exactly what am I being charged with here? What have I done wrong?"

"You struck a federal park ranger," she said. "Hands behind you, please."

Hale heard a delicate jingling as Terry snapped open the handcuffs to put on him. He stood straight and put his hands behind him. "Okay, I did strike you," he said. "But I thought you were with him."

"Who?"

"Somebody who did something a lot worse than I did. Look, I ejected from a plane. You must've seen the crash."

She snapped a cuff on one wrist. "Nope. I saw what looked like a plane, but—"

"That was me!" Hale said eagerly. "I mean, it was mine."

Terry snapped on the other cuff. "Tell it to the judge."

Hale turned suddenly and Terry stepped back. She raised the gun.

"Lady," he said, "you don't know what's going on."

"Obviously," she said, "but here's the situation as I see it. Wherever you came from, you're in my house now, pal. And since I don't know you from Job, you're under arrest until we get this sorted out. *Kapish?*"

Hale shook his head. "You are one mule-headed lady."

"You really know how to flatter a gal," she said.

"Listen, I need your help so I'm going to have to tell you something I can't tell you."

Terry holstered her gun and took Hale by an arm. "Save yourself the inner struggle. I don't want to hear it."

"You've *got* to," Hale said.

"Wrong," Terry countered. She put her hand around his elbow and started walking him ahead.

"Dammit!" Hale snapped. "There were nuclear weapons on the plane. Real ones, not dummies. We were on a training mission and the guy I was flying with is trying to steal them."

"Are you related to Mrs. Parker?" she asked. "Her son, maybe?"

"You don't believe me, do you?" Hale asked.

"You could say that."

"Jesus!" Hale said, exasperated. "You think I staged all this just to fool you?"

"No," she finally admitted, "but I honestly don't know what to think."

"Then let me tell you," Hale said. "I have to stop this guy, and I need your help. At least, I need you not to try and *stop* me. Please. I'm not crazy, and I promise not to try and hurt you."

Terry came around Hale and faced him. "Show me some ID." she said.

Hale rolled his eyes. "We don't carry any on missions."

She made a face. "Of course not." She pushed him. "Let's get going."

Hale stiffened his legs. "No."

She pushed the gun into the small of his back. "Yes."

"Go ahead and shoot," Hale said. "I'm not moving. I have to go after him."

"The mad bomber," Terry said.

"Right," Hale said.

"Listen to me," Terry said. "Come back to the ranger station. Clyde will contact your superiors and they can decide what to do."

The ranger gave Hale a rough push, and huffing with frustration, he used the forward momentum to jump up, tuck his knees into his chest, and slide his cuffed hands under his feet. Hale turned and snatched the revolver from her holster, and pointed it at her head.

The first indication he had that she'd whipped a knife from her belt was when he felt the point against his throat.

Friggin' scrawny moonlight, he thought. *Those things are supposed to glint.*

He looked at her with a half smile. "This isn't exactly a standoff," he said. "I've got a gun."

Terry said, "I know it isn't a standoff. I never keep my gun loaded."

She tapped her belt. He glanced down at the silver tips of the bullets. *They* glinted, damn them.

Terry held out her hand. Hale allowed the revolver to swing by the trigger guard on his finger and Terry pulled the gun away.

They were standing less than two feet apart. In the moment that Terry's eyes shifted to the gun, Hale hooked his left leg behind hers, wrapped his hand around her knifehand, and pushed her backward, over his leg. As she fell, he spun her around so that he landed on top of her, the knife she still held at her throat.

They hit hard and Terry lost her breath.

"Sorry about this," Hale growled in her ear, "but I'm telling you the truth."

She struggled for a moment, then gave up. "This is *not* a good way to convince me," she snarled, followed by another short burst of angry wriggling.

Hale said, "I think it is. I could kill you now, right?"

Terry didn't answer.

"*Couldn't* I?" Hale angled the tip of the six-inch blade against her jugular vein.

"Yeah," Terry nodded. "You could kill me."

"Okay," said Hale. "Now that we agree, let's talk."

The captain let go of Terry's hand and rose. He offered to help her up. She shook her head and stood on her own. She was still holding the knife.

"All right," she said, rubbing her throat. "Talk."

"Like I said," Hale told her, "I need your help to track and trap this guy."

"How?" Terry brushed herself off.

"Fake with a left so I can hit him with a right." He watched her for a moment. "Hey, I'm really sorry about all this. Did I hurt you?"

"I've survived hungry mountain lions, black bears, bighorn sheep, and mule deer." She threw back her hair. "You're a featherweight—to stay with your boxing metaphor."

In spite of his cracked skull and rage at Deakins, Hale smiled.

"So what do you want to do?" she asked.

"What I'm thinking is, we've got to get to a radio."

"I have one in my truck," she said.

"Good," Hale said. "We go there and you get on the radio, say I'm unconscious and you're bringing me in."

"Why bother? Why not just radio McMurran and let them know what's going on? Get the Marines in here."

Hale shook his head. "Deakins—that's the prick, Vic Deakins—will be monitoring any radio transmissions out of here."

"You sure?"

"Completely. He's thorough, will have thought of everything."

"Except this plan of yours," she said warily.

"Yeah," Hale replied. "The way he sent me out of the plane, the last thing he'll expect is for me—us—to be coming after him."

"Sounds like a great guy," Terry said. "Who is he?"

Hale looked down. The horrible betrayal went down like sour milk. "He was someone I would've trusted with my life. He's the last guy in the world I'd expect to do something like this. I still can't believe it."

Terry sheathed her knife, then looked around for the revolver. "Think he's in this alone?"

Hale shook his head. "No. He'll need help with the nukes. He has to have people on the ground. People and transportation."

"Yeah," Terry said as she found the gun. She started plugging bullets into the chambers. "I guess this isn't the kind of thing you could just go in and wing."

"No," said Hale. "He has to have been planning this for a while." He looked at the ground. "Why didn't he talk to me? Maybe I could've changed his mind."

When she finished loading the gun, Terry snapped her wrist. The cylinder flew shut. She holstered the revolver, then walked over to Hale. "If you couldn't have, would you have told your superiors?"

Hale looked at her. "I would've had to," he said. "For Deak's sake."

She shrugged. "Then that's why he didn't tell you." She opened the handcuffs. "You've given me a reason to trust you," she said. "I just hope I'm not setting myself up for the Sucker of the Year award."

"Don't worry," Hale said as she removed them. He rubbed his wrists. "That's one trophy I've got a lock on."

16

The round, green screen glowed in the darkness of cockpit of the Black Hawk. Rhodes had been watching the screen intently, dejectedly, for several minutes, staring at the electronic white grid overlay that shifted as his men moved eastward. Their own presence on the grid was indicated by a black rectangle.

Finally one and then another white blip showed up on the lower right corner of the screen.

"Got 'em!" Rhodes said into the microphone. He pointed them out to the pilot, and McKellar nodded.

"What are the coordinates?" Wilkins asked.

Rhodes checked the grid. "One's in M-17, the other's in M-18."

"They're both in a crevasse, according to the relief map," Wilkins said.

"How deep?"

"Looks like forty, forty-five feet on average," Wilkins told him. "Not too wide, either. If the bombs had landed widthwise, they'd most likely be lying across the top."

"We can handle that," Rhodes said. "I'll let you know what we find there. Over."

The dots came closer to the rectangle as the Black Hawk

homed in on the coordinates. Rhodes felt good about having found them, and he felt even better when they were within five miles and Lieutenant Thomas's Geiger counter told them, in its low, steady *click, click, click,* that the warheads seemed intact.

Twenty minutes later, the Black Hawk was resting on the edge of the crevasse. The men had hammered a piton into the hard rock and lowered strong nylon lines, which Rhodes— the only experienced climber—used to rappel down. Thomas and Reed shined powerful flashlights into the crevasse, while Kelly stood guard with a MP5SD silenced submachine gun.

The fissure was jagged, seven feet wide at its widest point, two feet across at its narrowest, and sudden outcroppings of rock slowed Rhodes's descent. After hitting bottom, he walked sideways, several yards to the right, where the crevasse narrowed.

He lit his own flashlight, shined it ahead, and smiled.

"General Wilkins," he said into his helmet microphone, "we've got one of them."

"How's it look?"

Rhodes played his flashlight around it, side to side and nose to tail. "Intact," he said.

"I copy," Wilkins said. "Thank God."

Rhodes looked up. "Gentlemen!" he shouted. "Let's move it along and find the other one!"

"We're with you, sir!" Kelly shouted down.

Rhodes moved gingerly around the smooth warhead, which had been dented and scraped as it fell. Though he couldn't stumble and jar it into exploding, he was anxious to show the sleeping serpent respect in its adopted home, lest he tempt its fire. As the dragon said of its new abode in Ezekiel 29:3, "My river is mine own, and I have made it for myself."

The officer followed the beams through the narrowing crevasse, chilled by the cold dampness and by thoughts of the disaster that, it appeared, they had barely averted.

17

When he was a kid, Clint McKellar loved Sweettarts more than any candy in the world. They came in flat foil packets—mixed fruit, grape, or cherry—and he inhaled the things. Made him hyper as hell, but who knew what sugar did back then?

Sometime between then and now, he'd outgrown their sweetness. Now he was a peanut butter cup man. There was something richer, more soul-satisfying about them. The candy rolled over his tongue, laying taste here and there, storing flavor in his teeth.

McKellar was sitting in the cockpit holding half a cup, a Colt M-16 rifle leaning against his leg, the rotor spinning smoothly, all right with the world, when he saw headlights to the left, by the rear of the chopper. Reluctantly placing the rest of the peanut butter cup in his mouth—experiencing a flavor over-dose, too much to enjoy at once—he grabbed the rifle and a flashlight and slid from the hatch in the side of the Black Hawk.

A Humvee pulled up alongside the helicopter as McKellar was still pulping the candy. The pilot shined the light on the vehicle.

The driver leaned out. "Hey, you guys need any help?"

"No," McKellar said firmly. "This is an Air Force training exercise, sir. I'm going to have to ask you to leave."

The driver pulled his head back in. "Hey, no problem. We just—"

His words were cut off by the *phut-phut-phut* of a silenced short-butt rifle which appeared in the rear window. His chest stitched across with gunfire, McKellar flew off his feet, half-spinning around before hitting the ground. Groaning, he tried to claw his way back to the chopper; a second burst, several ugly shots to the throat and head, stopped him. The pilot lay there with the flashlight shining in his face, illuminating his wide, dead eyes and the liquid chocolate running from his mouth.

"Nice shooting, Lett," said the driver. "What happened to taking people out with a nice, clean bullet between the eyes?"

"Shut up, Novacek."

Another Humvee pulled up fast and braked hard. Baker and Johnson got out, followed by Mr. Pritchett. Johnson was wearing a radio headset; the slender Pritchett was wearing a scowl. He stopped in front of the open hatch of the Black Hawk and surveyed the scene. Though he moved with slow, liquid movements, there was coiled anger beneath the tanned flesh.

Baker looked from McKellar to Novacek. "Any sign of Deakins?"

"Not a squeak." He looked at his watch. "But he's still got a few minutes."

"Not if he doesn't have good news for me," Pritchett said.

"Them sounds like fightin' words," said a voice from the darkness, affecting a Texas drawl.

The men fired looks toward the darkness behind the helicopter. Pritchett turned more slowly as a match flared, the tip of a cigarette glowed, and Deakins walked from the shadows.

"Were you threatening me, Mr. Pritchett?" he asked.

"Warning you," Pritchett said. "You assured me this would go smoothly."

"It is going smoothly, I assure you," Deakins said.

"Oh?" Pritchett snickered mirthlessly. "Our merchandise isn't where it was supposed to be."

"Ah, but we always planned on the search-and-rescue team finding the weapons for us," Deakins said. He pulled on his cigarette and exhaled dragon plumes through his nose. "And they have, Mr. Pritchett. I really have thought of everything."

Johnson had been standing well away from the helicopter rotor, pressing the headset to his ears. He joined the others now.

"News flash, gentlemen. Two gunships just left McMurran and they're headed this way."

Pritchett's displeasure turned to disgust. "I suppose you thought of that as well, Deakins?"

Deakins took another deliberate drag. "That, my friend, will take care of itself."

"How?"

"It just will," said Deakins. "Trust me."

"Trust you?" Pritchett said. His thin lips were tight and droplets of perspiration formed along the line of his slicked back blond hair. "I'm beginning to think that's unwise. Not that you aren't trust*worthy* . . . just inept. For instance, there's also the matter of the other pilot. We saw him eject. We saw the parachute open. We saw it drift to earth. Did you think of *that*?"

"First of all, you get a B- on your report," Deakins said hotly. "He didn't eject. *I* ejected him. And he wasn't exactly strapped in. But assuming he did land safely—and that's a pretty big assumption—you don't have to worry about Hale. He's not a threat. He's not a fighter. If he managed to stay in his seat, if he survived the fall, he's probably hiding behind a rock somewhere praying I don't find him."

Johnson took a step toward Deakins. "That may be, Deak. But I heard a park ranger call in. Said she saw something fall and was gonna go check on it."

Pritchett glared at Deakins, who stared at Johnson. Johnson looked at Pritchett and, flicking his Marlboro into the night, Deakins turned to Novacek.

"Better get the chopper ready. You can look for her when we've cleaned this up."

Novacek gave him a one-fingered salute then jogged to the hatch of the helicopter and climbed in.

"Christ," said Deakins, "doesn't anyone salute with a full hand anymore?" He looked at Lett and Baker, then nodded toward a crevasse some thirty yards distant. "I believe you two have a little work to do?"

"We'll have it wrapped up in a jiffy," Lett said.

Pritchett regarded him. Neither man spoke.

Lett finally said, "Is there something else?"

"Yes," Pritchett said. "Why are you still standing here?"

Lett said, "Sorry, Mr. Pritchett," and hurried off with Baker.

Deakins shared a steely, eyes-locked moment of silence with Pritchett, then turned and walked to the helicopter. He climbed inside, found Novacek busy pushing buttons and checking readouts in the cockpit.

"Just about ready," he said.

Deakins waited.

Novacek took a quick look at the night vision sensor, with its forward-looking infrared scanner. He made sure the elevation turret was operative, then rubbed his hands together.

"Ready," he said.

"No," Deakins said, leaning past him and flipping off a switch marked Com Link. "*Now* you're ready. Don't come back without a scalp, hear?"

"Loud and clear," Novacek replied.

Deakins left the chopper, and as soon as the hatch was shut

it was airborne, brushing the treetops, spotlights off, infrared on, searching for a truck, a lady ranger, and a man who would soon join the Black Hawk pilot swapping stories and battling enemies in Air Force Valhalla. . . .

18

Rhodes was passing through a snug turn in the fissure when his helmet headset suddenly sounded *solid*, as though it had been shut off.

He stopped. "Hello? McMurran?"

Nothing. Well, that did it, he thought. The headset *had* gone dead. He looked up, and was about to shout to Reed when he heard a familiar sound, like a hardball hitting a catcher's glove. He heard it three times, followed by the sounds of moving rock, followed by Reed falling into the crevasse and landing two feet ahead of him.

"Reed?" he said. "What the blazes—"

Rhodes shined his flashlight on the lieutenant, saw the bloody patches over his heart, then heard an array of *pop*s, like champagne corks on New Year's Eve, intermingled with dangerous-sounding *ping*s as bullets ricocheted off the rock around him.

With a howl, Lieutenant Thomas fell into the fissure a few feet ahead of Reed.

The *ping*s came closer, and though his mind was reeling, Rhodes's hand assimilated the bad news and doused the flashlight.

He pulled out his pistol, then froze as he heard the repeated kickoff crunch of boots on rock. Someone landed hard on the ground beside him.

"Sir?" someone whispered. "Sir, it's Kelly."

Rhodes hushed him and the bullets stopped. Sweat was pouring into his eyes and he removed his helmet. The lieutenant colonel remained still, listening for sounds from above. All he could hear was Kelly's fast, thick breathing to his right. A moment later, he could feel it as well.

A flashlight beam played over the jagged walls, seeking them out, and Rhodes gently cupped his right hand across Kelly's mouth, pressed him back against the rock. The officer breathed heavily through his nostrils. The light was approaching from Kelly's side. Raising his left arm, Rhodes waited; when the beam was directly on him, the officer fired.

Lett moaned and tumbled into the fissure. He stuck halfway up, lodged between two outcroppings, his head and arms dangling; his light and gun clattered down noisily.

Rhodes leaned very close to Kelly's ear. "How many were up there?" he asked.

Kelly held up three fingers.

Rhodes said quietly, "They've been burned. They'll be taking stock of things for a minute or two."

He turned on his flashlight, shielding the top with his hand to prevent its being seen from above. He looked ahead at the second weapon, which was lying some twenty feet away.

"You take the one behind, I'll take the one ahead," he whispered. "We'll open the access panels, put in a couple of grenades. The nukes won't go nuclear, but they will go dirty. I won't lie and say we'll be all right: we won't. But if we're gonna go, might as well take those bastards up there with us."

Rhodes looked into Kelly's eyes. They looked frightened but resigned. He patted the lieutenant on the shoulder, then turned to go.

78

"Just one thing, sir," Kelly said.

Rhodes stopped, turned. "What?"

The lieutenant flicked on his flashlight: in the other hand was a Beretta. "This," he said, putting six of the magazine's fifteen shells into Rhodes.

The lieutenant colonel flew backward, into the dark.

Finding him again with his light, and seeing the ruby life spilling from him, Kelly leaned his head back and shouted, "Done!" Then, moving back through the fissure, he returned to the rope, climbed, and rejoined his companions.

19

In his command post at McMurran, Colonel Wilkins sat around the table with his advisors, Majors Jett and Lee. They listened to the silence coming from the compact, digital, state-of-the-art, utterly helpless console.

The telephone beside the radio beckoned. If ego weren't an issue, if it weren't for the long-standing "we can handle this" attitude at McMurran, would Wilkins be sitting here while God only knew what was going on out there? Though part of him wanted to get a nuclear emergency search team to the site, a larger part of him didn't want to panic—or cause panic if the press learned that NEST was involved. The odds were that this was a blown fuse in the Black Hawk or a crapped-out chip in Rhodes's helmet, and not a leaking warhead.

Lee unclasped his hands and jiggled a coaxial cable in the back. Then he pushed the auto tune button. The computer-sized unit quickly ran through the audio spectrum to the immediate left and right of the channel. The silence was as thick as before.

"Maybe something happened to the relay inside the chopper," Jett suggested.

Wilkins said, "Wouldn't they try to contact us, then, on the walkie—"

"Colonel Wilkins?" a terrified voice exploded from the suddenly live speaker. "Sir, are you there?"

Wilkins leaned toward the unit. "I'm here! Who is this?"

"It's Lieutenant Kelly, sir."

"What happened, Kelly?"

"Colonel Rhodes is dead, sir," Kelly said. He swallowed audibly. "They're *all* dead."

"What happened?"

"It's . . . it's the nuke, sir," Kelly said. "It's open! Wide open!"

Wilkins looked at his advisors. Major Lee was already out of his seat and running toward the door.

"I'm going to the tower to recall the teams," he said.

Wilkins nodded.

"Oh, God, sir," Kelly waited, "what am I going to do? I was exposed!"

"Just stay where you are, son," Wilkins said. "We'll get help to you."

"But the radiation!" Kelly gurgled. "God, God . . . I want to have kids, sir. I . . . I feel sick."

There was a clunk, and then the radio went silent again.

Wilkins looked at Major Jett. "Get the Room on the line for me," the colonel said. "We're going to need NEST to handle this."

"Right away," Jett said, reaching for the phone.

Wilkins slumped in his chair. It was as though, one after another, every worst-case-scenario option was taking place. He couldn't have written a worse disaster.

It hadn't even registered, really, that Rhodes was dead. In Vietnam, he'd seen people die. The spurts of blood, soul-piercing shrieks, sudden disappearance of fingers, limbs, or faces—all of that wrote death in stone. But hearing about it like this, especially here in idyllic Utah, just didn't seem real. The sick irony was, if this was as bad as Kelly had indicated, more people were likely to die than had perished in any war or disaster in the second half of this century. And the nuclear arsenal of the U.S. military would be investigated, made public, and hamstrung for decades.

As he contemplated the scope of the unfolding disaster, Colonel Wilkins told himself that world-shaping events didn't always start with a bullet in the head of a president or the killer who stalked Archduke Ferdinand or a hard-boiled team of assassins gunning down the czar or some other hard target. Sometimes they began on the other end of a radio on a quiet night in a little corner of Utah.

For the first time, Wilkins found himself wishing that he had the capacity of poor Lieutenant Colonel Rhodes to pray. Because before this night was done, he had a feeling he'd need it.

20

Lieutenant Kelly emerged from the crevasse to applause from Major Deakins.

"You missed your calling," Deakins said.

The lieutenant bowed slightly as he approached. "I'd like to thank the members of the Academy and especially my father, who was always drunk and taught me how to act scared—"

"Save the comic relief for amateur night," Pritchett interrupted. He looked at Deakins. "You wriggled out of that corner, and I hope you've got another surprise up your Nomex sleeve. If I'm not mistaken, there are two attack helicopters headed this—"

"Not any longer," Johnson cut in.

Pritchett's eyes shifted to the radio operator. "What happened?"

Johnson tapped his helmet. "They've just been recalled."

Kelly swaggered over. "As I was saying, I wanted to thank my dad for teaching me to lie like a whore."

"They just turned around?" Pritchett snapped his fingers. "Like that?"

"Like that," Deakins said as he approached Pritchett. "You see, thanks to Kelly's performance, McMurran thinks they've got an exposed core or two down there. They'll want to get a satellite to take a look in the visible and various other spectra, but it'll take ninety minutes minimum to put one in position. Until then? Well, people get a little weird when it comes to radiation. No one'll have the balls to come here unless it's NEST."

Deakins leaned close to Pritchett.

"That's Nuclear. Emergency. Research. Team. Guys in spacesuits. The top bubbleheads are calling them in now, but the nearest team would need at least two hours to pack up, get to Utah, unload, and get out here. And we, being already here and well prepared, will need only an hour to reach our connection with the transport team. So relax."

Pritchett's expression hadn't changed. To Deakins, he still looked as wary as he had the day they first met and talked about this little adventure. Of all the scuzzbags at that meeting, Pritchett was the best dressed, tannest, and scummiest.

Deakins took a few steps away from his employer. "Now, Mr. P., if I may make a suggestion. It isn't that I'm not delighted with your presence. But the truth is, you really don't need to be here. It will be perfectly okay with me if you truck on over to the nearest greasy spoon and have yourself a cup o' Joe."

"I think not," Pritchett said. He added dryly, "It excites me to see a professional at the top of his form."

"Suit yourself," Deakins said. "Just don't get in the way, okay?"

"Okay. Oh, Deakins?"

"Yeah?" the major said over his shoulder.

"Just don't give me a reason." Pritchett smiled.

21

Terry and Hale were hurrying down the slope, Hale nearly outrunning his flashlight beam as Terry moved through the dark, behind him.

"Don't walk there!" Terry shouted as Hale's boots scrunched on terrain that sounded like stepped-on cornflakes.

"Don't walk where?" Hale asked.

"On that black earth."

He slowed, shined the light down. "The stuff that looks like burnt toast?"

"That's cryptogamic soil," Terry said. "It's very fragile. One footprint takes centuries to repair."

Hale stopped, stepped onto the rocks that lay alongside the path, and continued down. "That's a new one," he said. "Endangered dirt."

Upon reaching the truck, Hale stood by the hood. Now that he wasn't moving, he became very chilly very fast, especially along his back and armpits, where perspiration was locked into his flight suit.

Terry reached into the open driver's window and picked up the microphone. "You sure you want to do this?" she asked.

He nodded once.

Terry clicked it on. "Clyde?" she said. "You there?"

"Terry!" he said. "Where the hell you been?"

"I found the pilot," she said. "Had a tough time: he's unconscious. I'm bringing him in."

"Hurt bad?" Clyde asked.

"I can't tell," Terry said. "Get an ambulance. I should be there in twenty minutes."

"You got it," Clyde said.

Terry clicked off, seemed proud of herself. "I improvised the ambulance bit."

"Nice touch," Hale agreed.

"So," she said, "the game plan is, I bring you—"

Hale hushed her with a raised hand. They both stood still for a moment, and then Terry heard it, too.

"Come on!" Hale yelled, grabbing her hand and pulled her back toward the trail as the Black Hawk, its lights off, came diving at them from a cloud.

The chopper's two M-60 side-firing machine guns sparked to life, chewing holes in the truck, side and top, and sending glass in one side and out the other. Terry heard a *thucka-thuck* duller than the rest, suspected that that was probably the gas tank, then knew it for sure a second later as the truck exploded.

She felt the heat of the blast on the back of her neck, heard Hale swear as they sprinted up the trail.

"We've gotta hide!" he said after the string of oaths. "Is there a cave or tunnel, anything—?"

"Follow me!" she said.

They leaped to the west, off the trail and into a wooded area as the helicopter bore down on them.

"We've got to get up that slope," Terry said. She pointed to a long stone cliff some twenty feet high, sloped like a playground slide, with vertical rivulets and notches cut by aeons of freezing and expanding ice.

Hale looked back as the chopper bore down on them, its

searchlights on now, seeking them out. "Then I suggest we hurry," he said, pulling her ahead.

They scrambled up the cold, dry face of the cliff, Terry digging in her rubber-soled boots and getting a firmer grip than her companion.

"Come on!" she said, holding onto a jutting rock halfway up and extending her hand toward Hale. Terry helped him to her side, after which she sidled up along a jagged, diagonal split in the surface. Hale was a pace behind her, their way lit by the lights from the Black Hawk. Though the machine guns churned, the intervening trees protected them from the fire.

Upon reaching the top, Terry flopped down and scuttled ahead.

Hale finished climbing, dropped to his belly, and looked around. He couldn't see a rock, a tree, or her. "Hide *where*?" he cried as he surveyed the dark, flat terrain. "There isn't even a goddamn—"

"Come on!" Terry shouted again from somewhere ahead.

The *zing* of bullets against a nearby rock sent Hale forward, though he still wasn't sure where he was headed.

"I can't see you!" he yelled.

"This way!"

"What way?" he shouted back, just before he disappeared.

Now that he saw, or rather fell into what Terry had been talking about, Hale felt like a Beijing Opera acrobat he'd once seen. The acrobat had been lying flat on a diving board when another man jumped on the end and somersaulted off. His leap caused the board to spring, which flung the other man up, making him somersault off the end. He went over three or four times, in a tight ball, before landing on the shoulders of the first man, who had reached the ground a moment before him.

The only difference between that and this was that there was no diving board, no other man, and Hale wasn't an acrobat.

Also, the Chinese acrobat hadn't hit rock after rock on the way down.

Hale had crawled off the edge of a crevice and tumbled in, butt over head over butt. When he finally stopped rolling fifteen feet and many bruises later, he was sitting on deep sand.

Terry touched his aching shoulder. It was too dark to see her.

"Are you okay?" she asked.

"My day," he said, "is complete."

"Sorry about that. I thought you'd see where I went."

"It's all right," he said, rising. His joints popped and fluttered like party favors. "At least I didn't scream or yell 'Whoa, Nellie!' or anything embarrassing."

"Can you walk?" Terry asked.

"Been doin' it since I was a kid," he replied.

"Then follow me—this way," she said, taking his hand and leading him through a labyrinth of high, tight fissures.

Above them, the chopper beat a low, angry course back and forth, its lights playing over the fissures.

"Where are we?" Hale asked.

"It's called the Joint Trail," she said. "It's a flatland crisscrossed by a grid of deep fissures."

She went to the right, continued at a fast walk for nearly a minute, then cut to the left. The helicopter was no longer on top of them.

"How the hell can you see anything?" Hale asked.

"Hey," she said, "I'm a park ranger. I told you, this is my house. I know every corner of—"

Terry stopped suddenly and Hale walked into her. His chin struck the back of her head and he stepped back, rubbing it.

"What's wrong?" he asked.

Terry stood there for a moment, then said, "I hit my damn head."

"On what?"

"On a wall. I should've cut right, not left, back there. This is a dead end."

"You all right?"

"Yeah," she said. "Just promise me something?"

"Sure."

"Don't tell anyone I did that."

Hale chuckled. "I'm Eyes-Only cleared," he said. "I can keep a secret."

"Good," she said. Terry squeezed around him and doubled back. Then she went down the fissure to the right.

This path sloped slightly and passed through an area with an overhead ledge. Flopping against the wall, Terry said, "We'll be safe here. He can't see us."

Hale stepped away from the wall and looked up. She was right about that: whatever had cut these fissures had slashed this one diagonally. The only way they could be seen was if someone were standing to the left or right of them.

Hale was way out of his element here. He felt like Rick Marshall in *Land of the Lost,* going over a waterfall and ending up in a prehistoric world of geologic oddities and giant flying monsters. All that was missing was the monkey boy Chaka.

He was about to sit down and rest his battered limbs when the ground shook and an explosion stormed his ears and chest cavity.

"Hale!" Terry screamed.

A second and then a third explosion pummeled them.

"What *is* it?" she shouted as soil fell on them, followed by chunks of rock and sod.

Hale thought for a moment, back to the cargo they had been carrying.

"Grenades!" he rasped. "He's dropping grenades on the trail, trying to bury us!"

Though the chopper wasn't above them, a large section of ledge dropped down a few feet to Hale's right.

Hale said, "Is there anywhere we can climb out?"

"To the left," she said. "The fissure ends, but it's not as steep as the other one!"

"Then move it!" he said, pushing her ahead as the grenades landed closer and the walls on both sides shook violently.

The end of the fissure was as dark as absolute night, and touching it, Hale found the wall far steeper than he had imagined.

"Are you gonna be able to climb out?" he asked.

"Yes," she said. "It zigzags up, and there are a lot of footholds. But he'll see me—"

"I'm counting on it," Hale said.

He asked for the gun, and then told her what he wanted her to do. Terry protested that that would show the chopper exactly where they were—just as a grenade exploded less than twenty yards behind them. Only a bend in the fissure protected them from the blast.

"If we stay here, he's going to get us eventually," Hale said. "Now, go!"

With a boost from Hale to the first foothold, she began climbing the fissure wall. It took less than a minute for her to reach the top, propelled by an explosion that was nearer by half than the last one.

Upon reaching the surface, Terry held up her hands and ran toward the white circle of the chopper's floodlight. The Black

Hawk swiveled around, facing her, then descended and approached slowly.

"This has nothing to do with me!" Terry yelled. "I want out!"

The pilot, Novacek, leaned his head from the window. "Fair enough. Tell me where he is and I'll let you go!"

Terry lowered one arm and pointed toward the wrong fissure.

"In there!" she shouted.

In order to reach the fissure, the helicopter would have to cross over the place where Hale really was.

Pulling his head into the cockpit, Novacek dropped the chopper even lower and moved on his target.

In the fissure, Hale had his back against the wall, his arms raised, the gun pointed straight up.

The nose of the helicopter moved into view just twenty-odd feet up.

"Black Hawk, UH-60A," he was muttering as the forward part of the cockpit edged over the rim of the fissure. "In '87 they moved the pilot seat back about a foot."

He stared along the barrel at the front sight as the cockpit moved directly overhead.

"That puts him right . . . about . . . here."

In the twelve years he'd been in the military, Hale had never shot at anyone. Not that he'd had anything against it; the opportunity simply hadn't presented itself. Now that it was here, the feeling of power was major. This was an uppercut that, if it landed, was going to smart.

His mouth open, right eye shut, Hale squeezed off all six shots as the chopper glided over.

It seemed to Hale as if the Black Hawk itself were alive. Somewhere in the middle of the fusillade, the helicopter listed sideways and simultaneously began to drop.

"Got him!" Hale roared.

Above, Terry also shook a fist and gave a little cheer as the helicopter rolled over and began to fall. But her joy was short-lived, as it suddenly angled forward, nose down, diving right at her—as though the pilot had fallen against the control stick, pushing it forward. The chopper was still on its side, the rotor spinning perpendicular to the ground.

"*Shit!*" she screamed, scrambling across the flatland toward the fissure. She literally dove in, stiffening her arms and legs and bracing herself between the two sides of the fissure, sagging like a clothesline in an alleyway. She looked up as the rotor hit the top of the fissure, smashing and grinding against the rock.

The collision caused the blades to bend and stop spinning, but the torque of the powerful turboshaft caused the sixteen-thousand-pound helicopter to twist and rotate as if it were a giant blade. The tail swung up and over in a high arc, the four blades of the tail rotor spinning like a buzzsaw, heading right for the fissure.

Terry wasn't sure how far she was from the bottom of the fissure, but she knew that if she stayed where she was she'd be falling—in two pieces instead of one.

Letting go, she folded her arms around her head and tucked in her legs, landing on the sands an instant before the tail rotor slashed down through the fissure. Though her upper chest, arms, and shoulders hurt where she hit, she managed to uncurl herself and spread out flat. She could hear the tail section descending, kind of liked the fact that her last word had been *shit,* and waited for the death stroke.

She felt the knifing wind from the blades, heard the deafening chug of the motor, but nothing happened. She lay there for several seconds, heard rocks cracking, felt the wind come closer, and then realized that the tail section was wedged in the fissure.

"Terry!" Hale yelled.

She squinted into the darkness, couldn't see anything other than the sands being vacuumed up and about by the rotor.

"Terry, worm over! *Hurry!*"

Strong fingers tugged at her hand. Her legs were bent to the side and she pushed forward, following the hand ahead.

"Come on," Hale said.

He grabbed her by the wrists and pulled her forward. She helped, using the sides of her feet, and was in his arms and backing away from the rotor as it fell the last few feet to the ground. The smell of fuel was in the air, the noise deafening, as the slowing blades clanged against rock and batted up clouds of sand.

Hale continued to back away from the choking storm, Terry in his arms, as the rotor chipped sparks from the rocks. They landed in a puddle of leaking fuel, and a moment later the dark fissure flashed orange. Hale threw himself on top of Terry as the fuel ignited, flames shot up to the gas tank, and the helicopter exploded.

The fireball seemed to spring from the red smudge of dawn which was just appearing on the horizon.

"Jesus Christ!" cried Pritchett.

"Novacek," muttered Johnson.

"Dumb fuck," complained Deakins.

Pritchett turned to Deakins, who was standing beside him, watching the spectacle.

"We don't have to worry about the other pilot?" Pritchett said. "Then how come the helicopter crashed?"

Deakins said, "Pilot error."

Pritchett looked at him. "Perhaps your error—pilot?"

Deakins didn't react.

"Must've hit a canyon wall," said Kelly. "Y'think?"

Baker said, "Maybe sand got in the intake."

Deakins said, "Maybe. Or maybe Novacek wasn't paying attention to what he was doing." He turned to Pritchett. "You hired him. You tell me."

"I don't think it was Novacek," Pritchett said. "I could swear I heard gunshots, Deakins. Didn't you?"

"No," Deakins said. "All I heard were the M-60s."

The major lit a cigarette and walked to the pit, where Baker and Kelly were working on the first of the nuclear bombs. They were in the process of delicately removing the pointed, yard-long front section of the weapon.

Pritchett followed him. "Tell me again how I don't need to be here," he nagged.

"You don't."

"But you said you planned this carefully."

"I have," said Deakins.

"I see." Pritchett stood there tapping his foot. "So losing a helicopter was part of it?"

"It was factored in, yes."

"And how are we going to move the weapons now?"

Deakins said, "With trucks. That's why they're here."

"Ah, we move to the trucks now," Pritchett said. "Just like that."

Deakins looked at him. "Yeah. Just like that."

"Well, Major, just so you know—I spent a lot of money underwriting this, and frankly, you're beginning to shake my confidence."

Deakins smiled at him. The men were watching them. Deakins turned and smiled at them all.

"Mr. Pritchett, here, doesn't know much about nuclear weapons," Deakins said. "But he does know a lot about money. Worries about it *alllllll* the time."

Deakins looked at Pritchett again and smiled a friendly smile.

"Now, I appreciate just how much money you and your associates have invested in this operation," Deakins said. "But, see—that's what it is." Deakins rested a hand on Pritchett's shoulder. He squeezed. "A *military* operation. And you don't know diddlypiss about that." As Deakins squeezed harder, his smile faded. "I've been in the military for twenty years. Spent two of 'em at the War College in Montgomery. Planned and flew over a hundred missions in the Gulf."

"I have your c.v.," Pritchett said.

"Good. Because what I'm trying to say is, that is what I do."

Pritchett replied, "And what I'm trying to say is, I'm not sure you're doing it very well."

Deakins lifted his hand. He brushed imaginary dust from Pritchett's shoulder, then he patted the side of Pritchett's face. "You're not sure I'm going it very well?"

"No."

Deakins patted harder. "You have a great deal of military experience, do you?" He struck him harder still.

Pritchett raised his arm and used his wrist to block Deakins's hand. "No, Major. I don't. What does that have to do with anything?"

Deakins looked at him for a moment, then lowered his hand. "Well, Mr. Pritchett, let's see if I can clarify things for you. We're in a battle. And combat is a fluid situation. So you plan for contingencies, which I have. And you keep the initiative, which I will. But what you don't do is—can you guess?"

Pritchett said nothing.

"G'wan, give it a try."

Pritchett remained silent.

"*Bzzzztt!*" Deakins said. "Time's up. What you don't do, Mr. Pritchett, is share command. It's just never a good idea. So while you're the backer, I'm the boss. Got that? Rest assured that the boss understands the backer's concerns. You and your associates gave me a lot of money to mount this operation. But don't worry. They're going to get ten times the amount back if we succeed."

Pritchett drew air through his nose. "What do you mean *if* we succeed?"

Deakins slapped Pritchett's face lightly with each syllable. "I-mean-if-we-suc-ceed." He stepped back. "We've got the nukes, we're," he looked at his watch, "seventeen minutes ahead of schedule, and everything will be in place within two hours. As I've said from the start, the only thing I *can't* guarantee is that the assholes in Washington won't do something stupid, like think I'm bluffing and refuse to pay."

Pritchett said, "And if they don't pay? Are you really prepared to go to the next step?"

Deakins turned to Pritchett. The major's mouth was relaxed now, his eyes cold. "Primed and ready," he said. "If they refuse to pay, then the Southwest'll be a very quiet neighborhood for the next ten thousand years."

Finishing his cigarette, Deakins flicked it aside, then sat on the edge of the pit, grabbed the rope, and joined the other two men below.

Everyone but White House Chief of Staff Baird had decided to take a break from sitting in the Pentagon Situation Room and doing nothing but waiting and speculating. Giles was airborne, headed to the crash site via Gulfstream jet; General Creeley was stretched out on a couch in the adjoining waiting room; General Schneider was talking with one of the night secretaries, a Gulf War veteran who was young enough to be his daughter; and Joint Chiefs of Staff Chairman Dryfoos was on the phone with his advisors in a borrowed office.

Baird paused the *Blockout* game on the computer and looked at his watch for the second time that minute.

7:28. It was 4:28 in Las Vegas, still too early to call the President. Besides, when he finally called, Baird wanted to be able to tell him something other than that the Air Force had been coldcocked. He wanted to say that they'd taken the offensive—even though that was a rarity these days, when the press learned things before they did and put them on the defensive. It was even worse now than it had been just five years before, when he'd been a big city mayor. And it had been pretty bad back then.

He leaned back so he could see Creeley outside the door.

"How much longer until that satellite's in position?" Baird asked.

Creeley raised his wrist in front of his face. "Forty minutes."

Baird said, "I don't understand why we haven't got one any closer."

"Because," Creeley replied, "we don't usually spy on ourselves."

Baird's phone beeped and he scooped it up. "Yes?"

"It's Giles," said the caller. "I've been thinking."

"About what?" Baird asked impatiently. He wanted something to happen, not someone to think.

"What if this wasn't pilot error?"

Creeley wandered in, followed by Schneider. Schneider pointed to his ears and Baird put the call on speaker.

"Is this a rhetorical question, Giles, or do you have something?"

"I think I have something," Giles said. "In the last transmission from the plane, Major Deakins said that Captain Hale had lost it and made the plane crash. We assumed that meant pilot error."

"Giles, this is Creeley," said the general. "What else could it mean?"

"What if Deakins was trying to tell us that Hale *made* the plane crash?"

"Mister," the general said indignantly, "that's what I thought you were going to say. Let me set your mental processes on the right track before there's a career-stopping crack-up. Our pilots are scrutinized closer than luggage from Medellin. They just don't go bad."

"Besides," said Baird, "it doesn't make any sense. Why crash a B-3?"

Apparently unfazed by Creeley's screed, Giles said, "Because two nuclear weapons would be worth a hell of a lot more money than an Air Force pension. Crashing the plane means

100

we have to sift through the wreckage for clues, and that takes time."

Dryfoos had returned, along with two assistants. "To whom would these warheads be worth money?" he asked. "Son, there are easier ways for someone to buy nuclear weapons. You go to one of the old Soviet Republics. They'll fix you up with a couple for the price of a BMW."

"I didn't mean they'd be worth a lot of money on the open market," Giles said. "I meant they'd be worth a lot of money to us."

"I don't follow," said Dryfoos.

"What I'm saying is, how much would *we* pay to get them back?" Giles asked. "The United States. To make sure that they weren't used in this country."

Dryfoos no longer appeared so confident. He glanced at Creeley, who looked as if he'd swung too hard with his bat and hit himself in the back of the head. Schneider's arms were folded, and he didn't look happy.

"Hold on, Giles, hold on," Baird said. "General Creeley, those nukes have codes or something that prevent people from using them, don't they?"

"Of course," Creeley said, recovering slightly. "Absolutely."

"No one has these codes," Baird continued, "outside of the President and you guys."

"Right," said Creeley. "Access to those codes requires the highest security. Level Eight, at least. Pilots like Hale are Seven, tops."

Baird looked at him. "But, General, Deakins is an Eight."

Creeley looked at his computer monitor, brought up the crew dossier, and read Deakins's particulars. "You're right," he said. "That shouldn't have been allowed. Somebody got careless."

"I'll say," Baird said. "If Hale has him, he can beat or drug the codes out of him."

Dryfoos turned to one of his assistants. "Get me a psych profile on both men."

"Yes, sir," said the young man, who turned smartly and left the Situation Room.

Dryfoos said to his other aide, "Where's that NEST team now?"

The young woman looked at her watch. "They were scheduled to take off twenty minutes ago."

"Who's in charge?" Dryfoos asked.

"Colonel Hunt," she said.

"Get him on the phone," the chairman said gravely. He faced the speaker phone. "Mr. Prentice?"

"Sir?" said Giles.

"That was heads-up work, son. Nicely done. We'll let you know how it turns out."

"Thank you, Mr. Chairman," Giles said as Creeley and Baird sat a little lower in their seats.

25

Six soldiers sat behind serious expressions in the cabin of the C-141A StarLifter transport plane. They were strapped into jumpseats, and all were alert when they reached their cruising altitude and rugged Colonel Randolph "Fox" Hunt rose. A very distant relative of General Francis Marion, the legendary "Swamp Fox" of the American Revolution, Hunt moved like his namesake. Only young radio operator Simon Yam did not look up as his TAC-Sat secure telephone beeped.

"Listen up, sports fans," Hunt said. "As you know, most of the time these threats are bullshit. We've been out on a few of those calls, and I know how you hate being all dressed up with nowhere to go. Well, I can't tell you how happy I am that this particular incident came along. It is not—I repeat, *not*—bullshit. Word from the front is that this particular broken arrow has broken open. Our ETA in Utah is ninety-six minutes. Everyone use that time to triple-check the seams and seals of their E-suits. Randall, Hopkirk—I want you to check the sensors on the bird. Hecht, Hill, Lancaster—you three go over the equipment, test the batteries, the whole deal."

"Sir?"

Hunt's steel-gray eyes shifted to the radio operator. "Yes, Airman Yam?"

The young man rose and held out the phone, which was attached to a backpack resting under the seat. He said with a trace of awe, "It's Chairman Dryfoos of the Joint Chiefs of Staff."

Hunt smiled. Finally, the big guns themselves, the Guns of Navarone, needed his team. Hunt welcomed the chance to prove their worth, and he walked over smartly and took the phone.

"Colonel Hunt here."

"Colonel," said Dryfoos, "I wanted to take this chance to wish you and your men good luck, and also to warn you. There's a chance we might have a terrorist out there."

"Is there new information, sir?"

"No," said Dryfoos, "just some very real concern around here that one of the two pilots onboard the B-3 may have gone bad."

"Who were the pilots, sir?"

"Captain Reilly Hale and Major Vic Deakins. Do you know them?"

"Sir, I boxed Deakins once."

"Well, we don't think he's the perpetrator. What's your plan for this kind of contingency?"

"Sir, we look for booby traps around the site and in the warhead itself, post guards, and check likely sniper nests. Are you thinking that it's a lone wolf or a pack?"

"We aren't sure," Dryfoos admitted. "Just be ready for anything."

Hunt smiled. He glanced toward the back of the aircraft, at the "bird": the Bell JetRanger III that was securely fastened in the cargo hold, its rotor blades folded over, its tail rotor mast lost in the shadows.

"We're always ready, sir." Hunt smiled.

"Obviously," Dryfoos said, "if this isn't an accident, we want the perpetrator apprehended. More importantly, though, we want the situation defused—at any cost."

"Understood, sir," Hunt replied. "We've been waiting for this a long time, and we won't let you down."

After hanging up and returning the phone to Airman Yam, Colonel Hunt updated the team, finished his briefing, then sat back down to reflect on his match with Deakins.

It was about eighteen months before, and Deakins had won after rope-a-doping him. Hunt had been assigned to NEST after that, and had never been able to wangle a rematch, not even an informal one.

Hunt hoped that Deakins was the rotten apple.

Oh, how he hoped that.

26

Hale and Terry had climbed from the fissure back to where it split left and right. When she realized how close she'd come to being ribboned and charred by the blades and the blast, Terry had grown a little pasty-faced, her mouth sagging as though the muscles had been cut. But she'd recovered quickly. Hale usually found vulnerability appealing in a woman, but he had to admit he got a little warm inside when he watched this one haul herself out of his arms and help him up the side of the fissure.

Hale went as close as he could to the burning cockpit and peered inside. Then he ran back to Terry.

"He's dead," said Hale.

"I'd say 'well done,' but that'd be an inappropriate turn of phrase."

Hale looked at her. "You got a nasty streak, lady." He grinned.

"Only for people that try to kill me. Everyone else, we tolerate."

They caught their breath and watched as the wreckage of the Black Hawk continued to burn. Oil-fed black-and-red flames knifed into the rising sun.

Hale's eyes moved from the fiery ruin to the horizon, while his mind moved to the future.

"How do they get out of here?" he asked.

Terry said, "Get out? Mister, I don't think that helicopter's going anywhere."

"I mean the weapons. How do they get the weapons out of here? Deak'd have a backup. He'd be prepared." He looked at Terry. "What would you do? How would you get a couple of half-ton warheads out of here?"

"Well," said Terry, "if they've got trucks, they could take the four-wheel-drive trail."

"There's a trail just for that?"

She nodded. "Very popular with the Range Rover crowd. And—shit."

"What?"

"He *has* got trucks," Terry said excitedly. "Clyde told me on the radio last night that someone brought trucks through the Needles Gate. Suspicious ones." She smacked her forehead with her palm. "Damn, I'm so stupid! They must be military trucks."

"Probably Humvees," Hale said. "Four-wheel drive, tough as tanks. They'll go anywhere. Would he still take that four-wheel trail?"

"He'd have to. It's the only way out."

"Where is it?"

"Right past here," she said, pointing, "a frog hop to the south."

"And where does it lead?" Hale asked.

Terry said solemnly, "Out of here."

Hale looked at the gravel trail, thought for a moment, then flipped open the cylinder of the gun. The red of the burning chopper was reflected in his eyes. "Do you have any more bullets?"

Terry faced him. "Hold on. *You're* going after this Deak guy?"

"I have to."

"What're you gonna do, shoot out his tires?"

"No," said Hale. "They'd just reinflate. But I'll think of something."

Terry looked up into his eyes. "Isn't he going to have a lot of guns and stuff? I don't want to sound insulting or anything, but you're Steve Canyon, not Dirty Harry. You don't stand a chance."

Hale held out his hand. Terry sighed and popped the bullets from her belt. She handed them to him.

"You might be right," he said as he loaded the empty chambers. "But I don't have a choice. Those nukes are my responsibility."

Hale snapped the cylinder shut and noticed his hand was shaking. It'd been a rough day, but that would never do. He shut his eyes, took a long breath.

"You're not up for this," Terry said.

"I am. Meantime, I need you to get to a phone to call McMurran. Will you do it?"

"Yes, but—"

"Thanks," Hale said. He offered her his hand. "Thanks for everything."

She shook it. "You're welcome. But—"

"Don't worry," Hale said. "I'll be okay. Listen, do you have a twenty?"

She looked at him. "You want to borrow twenty dollars?"

"Yeah. I didn't bring my wallet. There's not much to buy onboard a B-3."

"What are you going to do with it?" she asked. "The gift shop's closed—"

"Funny," he said, then held out his hand again.

With a look of disbelief, Terry slipped her wallet from inside her jacket and gave him a twenty. "That's next week's grocery money," she said.

"I'm good for it," Hale said, squatting beside a rock.

"Not if you get dead," she rejoined.

"In that case, call Whiteman and ask General Hubert Boone for it," Hale told her.

"I'd rather you be here to pay me back."

Hale stopped what he was doing and smiled up at her. "That's the first nice thing I've heard all day. Thanks." He finished slipping the money half-under the rock. "But don't worry. I do have one thing going for me."

"What's that?"

He stood. "The last thing in the world Deak expects is for me to come after him." Hale's expression grew distant as the red of the fire became the blinding sting of a right hook. He felt himself stagger back as his vision grew clear and Deakins's face came back into focus. "See, I'm not a fighter. I don't have the fire in the belly. I give up too easily. At least, that's what Deakins says."

"Is he right?" Terry asked.

Hale raised an eyebrow and took a deep breath. "Maybe. We'll see." He held the gun by his face, pointing up. "Forget Dirty Harry. With the mad I've got on, Deak's gonna think he ran smack into the Terminator."

With a self-effacing wink, Hale turned to go. No sooner had he reached the trail, his mind vaulting from one bitter thought to another, than he heard stones clattering behind him.

Hale turned and saw Terry walking toward him, her arms swinging determinedly. He stopped.

"What are you doing?" he demanded.

"Coming with."

"No," Hale said. "I'm a soldier. You work for the Park Service. Go to a phone."

"The nearest one is a two-hour walk. Doesn't help us, does it? And I know this area. You're going to need my help."

"I can handle it."

"Really?" she said. "I know caves, mines, places where the position of the sun'll make it impossible for him to see you. You go off on your own like this, you're not a hunter. You're a hiker with a gun, about as effective as Dirty Dingus Magee."

Hale didn't think much of her metaphors, but she had a point. "You don't have to," he said.

She reached his side. "Some people running around with nuclear weapons? Yeah, I have to."

Terry had another point. "All right," Hale said, "but I'm the guy who lost the nukes. If there are any risks to be taken, I'm taking them. Understood?"

"Understood," she said. "Now, let's head for that cliff off to the west. It overlooks the Needles, which is probably where they'll still be."

Hale's mind was still a confusion of thoughts and emotions as they set off. But he was able to focus on one thing, at least: after all that had happened today, it felt good not to be alone.

27

Baker and Kelly had removed the front sections of the nuclear bombs, the business ends, and had slung harnesses under the two-hundred-pound sections. The harnesses had been hooked to cables that were attached to winches in the front of the Humvees. Carefully, Deakins moved one Humvee forward, pulling the warhead from the pit. Then he climbed into the second Humvee and gently dragged the second nuclear weapon from the pit.

With their metallic heads reflecting the red of dawn, the warheads were loaded into one of the Humvees. Then the tailgate was shut and Baker slipped behind the wheel of the weapons-carrying vehicle. To keep the weight down, he was the only one in that Humvee. Deakins climbed into the front seat of the other Humvee, beside Kelly. Pritchett and Johnson sat in the back and both vehicles started off, Baker in the lead.

Deakins lit a cigarette and let his head roll back.

Pritchett waved a hand in front of his face. "Do you mind?"

Deakins looked at Pritchett upside down. "I don't mind at all," he said. He handed the pack back. "Go ahead. Take one. On me."

Pritchett regarded Deakins. The major would have given

away a winning lottery ticket if Pritchett would act on what was obviously in his mind: to pull the cigarette from his mouth.

But he didn't. He just sat back, looking crabby.

As everyone else released their breath, Deakins collected his thoughts. He couldn't help but think about Hale. Part of him still wished he'd invited the captain to join him in this escapade. They could've had some fun together, both during and after the gig. He would have loved to introduce Mr. Constipated to some fun times in New York. Grab a couple of ladies and hop the Concorde to Paris for the weekend.

Shit, Deakins thought. *Tits to his left and right, and Hale'd probably want to go up front and fly the damn plane.*

But Hale was too uptight for something like this. Uptight and upright. Over the past four months, each time he'd been tempted to tell Hale about it, Deakins had stopped himself. He worried that even if Hale didn't join him, he'd empty his guts to General Boone.

What a poor, sorry fool, Deakins thought. Maybe it was the fact that Hale wasn't raised streetwise, or was over ten years younger, or was really satisfied being on the Air Force carousel with an inadequate pension for a brass ring. Deakins had signed up because he wanted to get out of Hell's Kitchen. He was tired of having to walk his little sister to the grocery on Ninth Avenue. To the laundromat on Eighth. He was no longer interested in small-change crap games behind the Lord Camelot Hotel and knife scraps after school.

But Whiteman wasn't far enough out of Hell's Kitchen, out of poverty. He was still trapped, no longer poor Aladdin, but the genie in the magic lamp, waiting to be released now and then. And that just wasn't good enough.

But he still felt bad for Hale. He was so damn naive. If he lived, Hale would never understand that in a couple hundred years, none of it would matter worth shit, however it turned out. He'd never see that what was truly important was grabbing each scrap of happiness while you could still enjoy it. And if people got hurt in the process, it was in the natural order of things. As a wise tyrant once said, if God hadn't intended for some people to be sheared, he wouldn't have made them sheep.

Hale would pity him, but the soap bubble in the backseat, that unimaginative priss Pritchett—he had nothing but cold contempt for Deakins. The major could feel it, like an open freezer door.

The good thing was, Deakins didn't like or trust Pritchett any more than Pritchett seemed to like or trust him. So the showdown, when it came, would be not be as bittersweet as the final fight with Hale.

If only Hale had cared enough to look after himself instead of other people, Deakins told himself. If only he'd learned how to get angry when he was punched, pissed off at the bootlickers who went farther with half his flying skills, frustrated with jerks like the assholes back in Texas or even Deak. If Hale had grown a real spine, Deak might have had a good man on his team instead of these hacks and semi-losers.

Poor, sorry Hale, Deakins thought, then smiled. *But soon-to-be-not-poor-me. . . .*

28

The Gulf Stream came to a quick stop on the tarmac at McMurran. An officer opened the door from inside and the steps folded down; as Giles hurried down them, Colonel Wilkins stepped up to meet him.

Giles rigidly extended his hand. "Colonel Wilkins? I'm Giles Prentice."

Wilkins's lips moved, but it took a while before words came out. "I, uh . . . yes. Welcome, Mr. Prentice."

"I know," Giles said as their hands locked. "I look fourteen. But I really do shave. Well, every other day, anyway."

Wilkins's forehead reddened. "Yes, of course. I'm sorry. It's just, your reputation makes you sound about fifty."

"I was born type A," Giles said.

Wilkins started back toward the command center, Giles slowing so as not to walk ahead.

"Any word from your search and rescue team?" Giles asked.

Wilkins shook his head. "Not a peep."

"I'm sorry," Giles said. "Has NEST picked up any radiation?"

Wilkins shook his head again.

"That's kind of strange," said Giles, "if there's an exposed core out there."

"Oh, there probably is," said Wilkins. "For whatever reason we're just not getting a reading. The ground may be soaking it up. It could be a lot of things."

They were quiet for a moment.

"So," Giles said, "you think I'm nuts about Hale trying to steal them?"

"Frankly, yes," Wilkins said. "Oh, I think you were right to run the idea up the flagpole. But I just don't see Hale—or any of our people, for that matter—doing something so insane." He chewed his upper lip. "Of course, just because I don't see it doesn't mean it can't be true. So on the off chance that you're right and everyone else is wrong, I've got ten attack helicopters fueled and waiting. If those missiles *have* been confiscated, the only way they're getting out of Canyonlands is in bite-sized pieces."

Giles nodded approvingly.

29

They heard the grinding of the tires before they saw them.

With a backward glance at Terry that reflected his concern, Hale ran the last few yards that separated him from the rock outcropping that overlooked the Needles. He dropped to his belly and looked down. Two Humvees were coming toward the northern cliff face, but not on the trail.

Terry lay down beside him, followed their course with her eyes. "Shit," she said. "They're taking the old rafter route."

"The what?"

"The rafter route," she said. "It's an offshoot of the four-wheel-drive trail. It was used by trappers up until the 1920s. They'd catch foxes in the northern hills and then head for the Colorado River and Lake Powell. They could go from here to Arizona to trade with the Navajos."

"Is that where Deak is going? To the river?"

"Looks like it," Terry said.

"What for? You said there was only one way out of here."

"I didn't think of the river," she admitted. "He can scoot out of here on anything from a log to a motorboat." She looked at Hale. "And don't say anything. I'm angry enough that I didn't think of it."

Hale grumbled. "I wasn't going to say anything. Getting upset isn't going to help us."

"True enough," Terry said.

Hale wasn't upset, but he did feel helpless as a baby as he watched the Humvees roll past them over two hundred feet below.

Terry suddenly jumped to her feet. "Come on!"

"Where to?"

Terry started running along the ledge. "I know something that might help."

"What?" Hale asked. His knee popped as he got up too quickly. "Even if we run, they're going at least ten miles an hour. We'll never be able to intercept them."

"Yes, we will," she said. "We're not taking the trail."

"What *are* we taking?" he yelled as he followed her.

"A shortcut," she said. She stopped by the eastern wall of the cliff.

Hale looked down the nearly sheer face. "This is a short-cut?"

She knelt, facing away from the cliff. "There are a lot of handholds, we've got the sun on us so we can see, and they won't pass by for at least ten minutes." She leaned on her elbows and backed over the side, putting her feet on a rock lip. She glared back at Hale. "It'll be like going down monkey bars. Now, you want to waste time or you want to get your nukes back?"

Hale didn't know whether he was having a charmed day, when nothing could hurt him, or whether he was about to press his luck. In either case, Terry was right. He hurried over, got on his knees, and followed her down.

Terry was wrong. It wasn't like monkey bars: it was like walking to your seats in the theater, seats in the center of a row where everybody else was already sitting down. With the added pleasure of being very unsure that the floor was even

117

going to hold up beneath you. These were rocks that hadn't been climbed on since the Ice Age, and the fragile footholds complained when Hale put his weight on them. He didn't for long, moving down quickly, at one point nearly stepping on Terry's hand as she descended.

The descent was slower than Terry had apparently anticipated, and as Hale began to fear that the Humvees would pass before they arrived, he shouted down that they should move faster.

Even as they did, he watched the Humvees approach and knew that there was one way they were going to catch them.

30

"Are you a fan of boxing, Mr. Pritchett?" Deakins asked.

Pritchett looked like he'd walked into a cheese shop by accident. Every line of his face registered displeasure. "I think it's barbaric."

Deakins said enthusiastically, "Me, too! I love it!"

"Please," said Pritchett, averting his eyes.

"No, really. Two men trying to do as much damage to each other as they can. That's as basic as you can get, don't you think?"

"What I think," said Pritchett, looking out the Humvee's side window, "is that it should be banned."

"So do I," Deakins said. "God, wouldn't that make it more exciting. Having to go into dark alleys and basements to see a bout—like cockfights and snuff films. You could smoke there, drink, no Dudley Do-Rights looking out for your health, physical or otherwise." Deakins lifted the microphone from the dashboard. He fired Pritchett another glance. "I bet we see eye to eye on a lot of things, Mr. Pritchett. What do you think?"

Pritchett didn't answer, which told Deakins exactly what the stuffed shirt thought. Deakins clicked on the microphone.

"Max," he said, "you there?"

A moment later, a crusty voice said, "Rodriguez and Sons, Fresh Produce, are here. Chickens are our specialty."

Deakins said, "Exactly where is 'here,' Maxie?"

"Sheppard and I are just pullin' up to the transfer point right now," he said.

"Good. How's your cargo?"

"Fine," Max said. "Shep'll get in there in time."

Deakins looked at the clock beside the radio. "We've got a thirty-minute cushion. See you soon. And Max? Remember— you don't get your lettuce unless I get my chicken egg. Remind lettuce *head* of that."

"I won't forget," Max chuckled, "an' I won't tell 'em you said that, either."

"Aw, go ahead," Deakins said. "Anger is one of the two things that keep people on their toes."

Max said, "All right—I'll bite. What's the other?"

"Greed," said Deakins. "Money, a woman, a political office—you're hungry for something, you'll do what it takes to eat."

Max promised to share the colonel's philosophy with the "lettuce head," and then Deakins hung up. As he did, he noticed Pritchett scowling in the back.

Deakins folded his arms. "You have a problem, Mr. P.?"

"Yes," he said. "You were talking about your plans on an open line."

Deakins said, "Yeah. So?"

"So what if someone was monitoring your communication?"

"Like who?" he asked. "The Air Force doesn't monitor radio communications, Max didn't use my name, and for all anybody who *might* have overheard knew, we were arranging to buy or sell some veggies."

"The rangers might have heard," Pritchett said, "and they aren't as stupid as you think."

"You're right," said Deakins, "they aren't stupid. That's why

Maxie set up Rodriguez and Sons. So he could move all kinds of shit through the great American Southwest." He leaned an arm on the back of his seat and smirked. "Any other critiques, boss?"

"Yes," he said. "I don't like you. Not a bit."

Deakins appeared wounded. "The good news is, that's not going to affect the performance of my duties. The bad news—for me, anyway—is that I really wish you did like boxing. Because when this is all finished, there's nothing I'd enjoy more than getting you in a ring and beating the ever-loving crap out of you." He smiled. "Think about it: I might give you a discount for the privilege."

Even in the ruddy darkness of dawn, Deakins could see the ire in Pritchett's eyes. And he cherished each passing second, as it brought him closer to the moment when he could hand this jerk his swelled head.

As Deakins was busy picturing the various ways he could do that, he looked out the window. The Humvee was just rounding the corner of a cliff. Beyond it, he could see the glimmer of sunlight on the majestic lake, which ran from southwest to northeast for over one hundred miles.

And then there was a resounding *clump* above him, and Kelly swerved away from the cliff as rocks and then a foot thumped down on the windshield.

31

Hale was ten feet from the ground when he decided to jump.

The captain stopped, tucked the gun inside his jumpsuit, and let the unsuspecting Terry shimmy out from under him. Then, a moment before the second Humvee passed by, he pushed off the cliff.

"My God!" Terry screamed as he fell past her.

Hale had chosen the second Humvee because if he'd jumped at the first and missed, he'd have rolled off the roof and under the wheels of the second. Hale landed facing the passenger's side, squatting, along with the rocks he'd been holding onto. When Kelly swerved, Hale was thrown toward the side and would have gone off, headfirst, if Terry hadn't landed beside him. She pulled him back by the collar of his flight suit and he landed on his butt.

"You're insane!" she screamed.

Hale didn't argue. The Humvee swerved back toward the cliff, Terry lay flat, and Hale got on his hands and knees, spreading them wide as he took out the gun. But before he could make his way to the driver's side, bullets punched up through the roof. The gunfire cut a connect-the-dots line between Hale and Terry, at one point missing her right elbow by an inch.

Terry pulled her arms in and was heads-up enough to get onto her side, making herself less of a target. A second volley followed, directly behind Hale. As he scurried forward to escape the attack, the driver swerved again. Momentarily off-balance, Hale thumped to his side on the edge of the vehicle, lost his gun and his balance, and skidded off the Humvee.

"Ter—" he shouted, biting off her name as he hit the ground hard.

A bullet split a rock on the cliff just above his head, raining particles into his eyes and mouth. Spitting out pieces of rock, he got to his feet and ran after the Humvee.

"Terry!" he yelled as bullets whizzed past. *"Terry!"*

Suddenly, the second Humvee stopped. Terry slid across the roof but didn't fall. The guns stopped firing. And then the wheels spun madly in reverse, churning up cyclones of dirt, and the Humvee rocketed toward Hale.

He threw himself against the cliff. Fingertips bleeding, muscles cramping, he climbed, dug in with his hands, and pulled up his legs so they were just above roof level as the rear fender grazed the cliff. The Humvee bounced off, rocking Terry, who leaped on the gun as though it were a fumbled football, to keep it from flying off.

Hale's grip weakened, he dropped when the Humvee passed, and then he was between both vehicles. The one in the front was waiting, blocking his escape, its braking lights aglow like the bloody mouths of many-headed Cerberus guarding the gates of Hell. The second Humvee stopped with a jolt less than ten feet away. It idled. Flashed its lights. Then waited.

Hale rose painfully, though the ache in his limbs was nothing compared to the hurt in his heart. The sun threw a red light on the faces of the men in the front seat, and he saw Deakins in the passenger's seat. He was talking into the car radio. Was that a smile or a grimace on the face of his longtime friend? he wondered.

Hale stood there, transfixed by the face of the Gorgon, unable to move even as he heard the engine rev and the tires spin behind him. He wasn't sure he *wanted* to move. If you couldn't trust your flying partner, your cockpit brother, a man who was as close to you as your own damn skin, what was there to live for?

"Here!" Terry shouted.

Hale snapped from his sullen reflection. Something slid across the Humvee roof and flew at him, spinning barrel-butt-barrel-butt.

It was the gun.

The sunlight also lit the ranger's face. It was anxious, dirty, more golden than red. It was also imploring, urging him to move.

All of this registered in the time between heartbeats. Hale bolted forward and caught the gun, stole a quick look behind him, and leaped up as the Humvee was about to mash him.

The tanklike vehicle struck him on the back while he was still in the air. He was rattled, hard, but he landed on the rear fender, facing backward, and managed to stay there by grabbing the flat metal sideguard on the left.

Hale raised the gun. The rear Humvee was nine feet away, eight feet, seven—

The captain fired and Baker screamed, then ducked. Deakins didn't move as the bullets crashed against the windshield, directly in front of his face.

Bulletproof! Hale swore.

The Humvee that Hale was on stopped close enough to jump a dead battery. Hale hopped off and ducked between the vehicles.

Deakins cranked down his window. Baker climbed from the

124.

first Humvee, an assault weapon tucked under his arm. He stepped out and aimed the gun at the roof. At Terry.

"Give it up, partner!" Deakins shouted. "Now, before we lobotomize Boo Boo Bear."

Silence. Baker edged toward the front of the vehicle. He saw nothing, made an impatient sound, continued forward.

"I'll give you a count of three, Captain," Deakins said. "One . . . two. . . ."

"Three," Hale said from behind Baker.

Baker didn't fire. He stood there as Hale, his chest filthy from having crawled around the Humvee, rose behind him.

Baker smirked. "Seems we've got ourselves a little stand-off."

Hale smirked back. "Not really."

Hale simultaneously fired two rounds into the back of Baker's head and smacked the barrel of the assault weapon down with his free hand. Kicking the dead thug forward, he wrested the gun from him, yelled for Terry, and ran around to the passenger's side.

Terry scampered from the roof to the hood to the open driver's side door of the lead Humvee before Deakins or Baker could turn a weapon on her. Before she even shut the door, she'd shifted gears, pushed down on the gas pedal, and was tearing along the old trail.

"You killed him!" Terry gasped.

"I don't think he was entirely clear on how stand-offs work. Anyway, he wouldn't have hesitated to waste you."

Terry looked in the rearview mirror as the second Humvee roared defiantly and started after them.

"Will they shoot?" she asked.

"These things are too well armored," Hale said. "And you saw about the windshields. Besides"—he grinned—"we've got the nukes."

Terry's eyes became huge as she hazarded a quick look back. "Ho-lee *shit!*"

"Don't worry," Hale said. "They're not going to explode no matter what happens."

"You sure about that?"

"Totally," he said. "But they could get damaged, and Deakins doesn't want that. So he'll treat us gingerly."

Terry's eyes grew a little smaller, but not much. "I'm chaperoning nuclear bombs. This is crazy."

"What's life without some excitement?"

"Relaxing," she said.

"We all get to relax soon enough," Hale said. "The long, long dirt nap."

"Great," she said. "I'm riding with Aristotle."

"Just sharing some of my accumulated wisdom," Hale said.

"Don't," she said. "It's depressing. Think happy thoughts, like in *Peter Pan.*"

"I guess that's why I used to box with Deak," Hale said, more to himself than Terry, "even though I got the crap beat out of me. It's better to feel something, even if it's a fist."

He slipped a thumb and index finger into his vest pocket and pulled out his sunglasses. The dark lenses fell out in small pieces. He tossed the golden frames to the floor and brushed the pieces off his lap.

"I just bought those, too," Hale said. "A flier without his shades—now I'm really defenseless." He looked back, squinting into the sun to make sure Deakins wasn't gaining on them.

"How are we doing?" Terry asked as she deftly cornered a turn close to the cliff.

"You know these roads better than they do," he said. "But we still have to lose them. How long until we reach the river?"

"About three miles," she said. "But the way this road goes, there's nowhere to hide. They'll see every turn we make."

"That won't help them if they can't follow us," Hale said.

Terry stole a look at him. "What do you mean?"

The pilot climbed over the back of the seat. He crouched beside the bombs. "I'm going to whip up a little distraction."

"Oh, good idea," Terry said. "Set off one of the nukes. That'll get 'em."

"That's not what I'm doing," Hale said. He poked through the equipment in the rear of the Humvee. "Deak would've been well prepared, which means—aha!"

With a triumphant flourish, Hale unscrewed the wingnuts from a bracket and lifted a plastic container of gasoline. He set it beside his foot. There was a toolbox in a well beside the bracket and he opened it.

"Round one, Deak," he said as he pulled a roll of gaffer's tape from the box. "Round two, us. Round three—"

"Us?" Terry said hopefully.

"Us," Hale said as he unwound a foot of tape and tore it with his teeth, "with a little help from Vyacheslav Mikhailovich Skryabin."

"Who?" Terry asked as she rounded another turn, this time more carefully.

Hale took a flare from the tool kit and taped it to the side of the can. "Skryabin, a.k.a. Molotov," he said. "The cocktail guy."

"Jeez," said Terry. "I didn't think they taught things like that in Survival School."

"They don't," he said. "I got this from a Tsui Hark movie."

"A what?"

"A Chinese gangster film," he said.

"We move in different cultural circles," she said.

Hale took a moment to double-check his handiwork. "Well, it isn't an official Molotov cocktail. But the results should be the same."

Hale picked his way around the nukes to the back of the Humvee, then popped the back hatch.

"Slow down," he said.

She let up slightly on the gas. Hale ignited the flare and leaned out the back.

"Slower!" he yelled as the wind tore at the flame. "Almost stop."

Terry gradually pressed on the brake pedal. The Humvee slowed amid a swirl of dust, and Hale leaned out. He laid the container on the trail.

"Now *go!*" he shouted. "Fast!"

Dirt and grass spit from under the wheels as Terry took off.

32

Kelly was watching the Humvee. He rounded the curve, and when the enemy slowed down he sped up.

"Gotcha!" he said as he tore down the straightaway.

Deakins wasn't looking at the Humvee. He saw the flare, saw the bubbling, melting plastic beneath it, and saw the gasoline pour from a smoky hole in the container's side.

"Stop!" he yelled.

Kelly didn't respond soon enough. When he finally mashed down on the brake, the Humvee skidded to a stop just yards from the container, and everyone but Deakins bailed out as it exploded. A geyser of fire shot up nearly twenty feet and came down in waves, burning the scrub grass, charring the face of the cliff, and engulfing the hood of the Humvee.

Inside, Deakins coolly climbed into the backseat, reached into the rear, and grabbed the fire extinguisher. He kicked open the back passenger's side door—his only display of anger— walked around front, and quietly and efficiently doused the flame.

When there was nothing but foam and white smoke on the front of the Humvee, the others ventured back, Pritchett ahead of Kelly and Johnson.

"I can't wait to see how this fits into your plan," Pritchett said. Then he added for good measure, "Commander in Chief, sir."

Deakin's cool veneer burned off, like the coat of paint on the Humvee's hood. He fixed Pritchett with a white-hot stare and stalked toward him. He held the extinguisher by its operating level. The red metal canister swung dangerously at his side.

Pritchett didn't retreat. Deakins stopped when they were nearly belt buckle to suspenders clip.

"Did you happen to notice what Hale did to Baker?" Deakins asked.

Pritchett said, "It was difficult to miss. Likewise that bug bomb he cooked up for us."

Deakins moved even closer. Now they were nose to nose. "That's very true, Mr. Pritchett. So's this. If you tweak me again, just one more time, you're going to *beg* to have your chips cashed that quick. You got that?"

Pritchett didn't answer. But he shrank back slightly, which was all the answer Deakins needed. The major threw the fire extinguisher at the cliff. The cylinder cracked and hissed as the remaining soda acid lathered out.

"Kelly," Deakins said, "see if the bullshit's true, if these things really can drive through Hell and back."

Kelly ran over to the Humvee. He opened the hot door with his foot, slid in, put it into forward and reverse, then tested the gas and brake.

"It works," he said.

"Then let's get our toys back," Deakins growled.

As he walked toward the Humvee, Johnson fell in beside him.

"Don't you think we ought to do something about Baker?" Johnson asked.

"Yeah," Deakins said as he climbed into the passenger's side. "Fill out the forms for sainthood and make him patron of all the dumbshit assholes who let second-rate wusses sneak up behind them and blow their friggin' brains out. Now, get in."

Deakins slammed the door. After giving Pritchett and the startled Johnson enough time to get in but not close the doors, he motioned for Kelly to move out.

Despite what had just happened, Deakins was angry but not unduly concerned. He knew Hale almost as well as he knew the dialogue from his favorite film, *The Wild Bunch*. He knew just what the guy would, try, every tired punch, and he also knew how flustered Hale would get when a few of them failed to connect.

And then he was going to enjoy reeling the big, dumb fish in. When he did, their history together notwithstanding, he was going to scale him alive for this inconvenience.

33

"I'm really impressed," Terry said to Hale as they zoomed away from the thick column of smoke.

"It was easy," Hale said. "I just figured out the thickness of the plastic container when I taped the—"

"No," she said, "I mean that you knew Molotov's real name. Most people don't even know Sting's real name."

Hale smiled. "That comes from being raised in a Texas household where my dad used to read us the newspaper at dinner. They hated Communists almost as much as Santa Ana." He looked back at the fast-dissipating smoke. If the Humvee were still working, Deakins would be after them. "We need a place to hunker down for a while," Hale said. "Got any suggestions?"

She thought for a moment. "There's an old copper mine about four miles from here—no road, just low hills that don't hold tire tracks very well. If we can get out of their sightline, they'll never find us."

"Sounds good," said Hale as he tried to use the radio. He tried several times to press the button that scanned the frequencies, but nothing happened. "Shit. They hardwired in their frequency. We can't call out."

"This Deakins seems to have thought of everything."

Hale nodded. "There's a lot of bad stuff I can say about him, but not planning ahead isn't one of them." He sat back. "Still, no one can plan for every contingency. And somewhere, somehow, he had to have missed something."

"You hope."

"Actually," Hale said. "I pray."

As Terry sped across a field and into the hills, Hale rolled down the window. The rising sun had begun to heat up the day, and the warm, fresh air felt good—better than it had when he was hanging on the face of the cliff.

Looking around, Hale knew he spent too much time in the air or on the base. The colors out here were sharp-edged and textured, the sounds were big and open, the smells were fresh—not machine-blown air and pine-tree locker room fresheners.

Or were his senses heightened, he wondered, because he was afraid that each of these sights and smells might be his last?

The mine was located where two hills met—or where some ancient fluvial erosion had cut one great hill in half. It was a Disneyland mine: craggy walls glittering with quartz on the outside, old timbers helping to support the entrance. Set back in the face of the hill were rusty metal doors with a padlock.

"This place was barely squeaking along for years," Terry said as she pulled up right in front of the entrance. "They shut it down when they hit an underground river. I thought we could hide the bombs in here."

"We may not have to," Hale said, getting out. God, the air tasted good here.

Terry turned off the ignition and joined him in back of the Humvee. "Then what are we going to do?"

Hale pulled down the tailgate, reached in, and fished around in the toolbox. "I'm going to take away their reason for being here."

As Terry watched, Hale knelt on the open tailgate and unscrewed a panel cover on the side of one of the B-83s. He removed it, exposing an LCD display, a clock, and a numeric keypad with large, brightly colored keys.

"Fisher-Price makes nuclear weapons?" Terry remarked.

"These keys are designed to be used in Alaska by people wearing heavy gloves."

"Oh," she said with an apologetic smile.

Hale punched a key which caused the LCD display to light up. "These nukes have fail-safe security codes," he said. "If you enter the wrong code three times, the nuke goes dead—all the circuitry shorts out and shuts down."

"Just like the security systems for car radios and ATMs," Terry said.

"Right," said Hale. "Those are spinoffs of Pentagon technology."

"And people say the public doesn't benefit from defense spending."

Hale looked at the LCD with satisfaction. "Could you hand me the radio?"

While Terry went around to get the microphone, Hale removed the panel from the second weapon. As he set it aside, he noticed a black plastic tag sticking out from beneath the weapon. He bent over it and gently tugged it out.

"McCann, David," he read aloud, "St. Jude's Hospital, Radiology Department." There was a strip of film across the bottom.

"What did you say?" Terry asked as she came back with the microphone. The wire was stretched nearly to the limit.

"Where's St. Jude's Hospital?" Hale asked.

"Salt Lake City," Terry said. "Why?"

Hale leaned back on his heels and took the microphone. "Because I think I know what Deak is planning."

The captain pushed the Talk button. There was a lump of

something in his throat, like when he used to call girls to ask them for dates. He hoped he was up to this, trading shots with the New York fast-talker.

"Deak, are you there?"

Silence. Wrong approach. He had a better idea.

"Ding, ding, ding, Deak," Hale said. "You hear that, Joe Palooka? We're starting a new round, and guess what? I've got you on the ropes."

There was a distinctive click from the speaker. Hale could feel Deakins's presence before he heard him.

"Well, hello," Deakins said. "Or maybe I should say, 'Hale and farewell,' because you haven't got me on the ropes and you never will."

"Huffin' and puffin', Deak, that's all I hear. I know you're stalling while you break out the radiation detector scanner and try to fix my location, but you're gonna be too late. Want to know why?"

"Please. Share with the class."

Hale held the microphone to the keypad as he started tapping in numbers. "Because I'm entering the wrong code, you scum. A couple more entries and these nukes are gonna be useless to you."

Deakins whistled. Hale felt a chill.

"Whew, you really got me there," Deakins said. "I sure didn't think of that."

Hale slowed down. He looked at Terry. Before, there had been a twinkling of relief in her eyes. Now it was gone.

"All that time we spent in the cockpit together, in the ring," Deakins said, "and you think I'm stupid? Jesus, give me *that*, at least. I got some new boards and circuits from a friend at Pantax. Cost me a year's wages, but what the hell. It's only money. And guess what?"

Hale didn't bother to guess. He knew the answer.

"If you don't stop screwing with the buttons, you may just

135

activate the warhead. Short countdown, sixty seconds, then boom."

Hale balled his free hand and squeezed until his nails dug blood from his palm.

"But nice try, partner," Deakins said. "You really gave this one more than I expected."

"Yeah?" Hale said through his teeth. "Well I'm not finished yet."

"Of course you are," said Deakins. "You're cooked, booked, and tottering on the brink."

"Maybe, but I know what you're planning."

"Do you, now?"

"Yeah," said Hale. "You're gonna ransom Salt Lake City."

Deakins snorted. "Am I really? What makes you think that?"

"That's where St. Jude's Hospital is. You're gonna hide the nukes in the radiology department so they won't show up on any NEST or satellite radiation detective scans."

Deakins said, "Wow. Now I *am* impressed."

"How much're you going to ask for?"

"Enough," Deakins assured him. "I've got a broker in Stockholm. Handles rock stars, politicians, drug dealers. Monday morning, he's going to buy me five percent of Volvo. For the rest of my days, I'm going to live off the dividends, happy in the knowledge I'm helping to build the safest car in the world."

"Money?" Hale said. "You're just doing this for money? I'm disappointed."

"Why would you do it? Wait—I know. You'd demand that Congress give carte blanche to NASA for a moon base, trips to Mars, fancy new airplanes to fly. I could go along with that—though I'd rather be personally rich. I mean, put yourself in my boots. What would you do?"

Hale said, "Kill myself."

"Now, now," Deakins chastised him. "That's your left brain

136

talking. Think right brain. Or is it the other way around?" Deakins said. "I can never remember."

Terry came over and pointed to Hale's watch. "The radiation scanner," she mouthed. There was anxiety in her expression.

Hale shut his eyes and nodded. He knew that time was tight, but this was Deakins. His old friend Deak, with whom he'd always talked about everything. This had gone way further than it should have, but maybe it wasn't hopeless. And if there were a chance, he had to take it.

"Deak," Hale said, "I want to do something."

"What?"

"Talk," Hale said. "Let's white flag it for an hour. You and I can meet, wherever you want."

"Sorry, no. I appreciate the sentiment, though. I really do."

"But *why* do this?" Hale yelled. "Or let me tell you. Because I got passed over for promotion, I'm going to show the bastards that I'm smarter than them all. Because everyone's selling out and cashing in, I might as well get my share. Because my parents abused me. Because my ex-wife was sleeping around."

Hale moved his mouth closer to the microphone. His voice was getting louder.

"Everyone's got reasons, Deak. We hear them on Court TV every day. *Because* I ate too much sugar. *Because* Mondays really depress me. *Because* the videotape I wanted to rent was out. It's all bullshit, Deak. There's no difference between you and the guy who shoots up the schoolyard with an M-16. You both think you have reasons. You both think you were wronged. But you want to know the truth?"

"I tingle with expectation."

"The truth"—Hale was practically screaming now—"is that you're both totally screwed in the head. You want someone to powder your behind, when what it really needs is a good, iron-toed kick."

137

Deakins applauded. "Then you accept the nomination for God Almighty?"

"Don't you have that backward? Aren't you the one planning to lay waste to a city?"

Deakins said, "Like I told you, I'm all for the God that smiteth." He sighed. "You know, Captain, I actually once thought of asking you to join me on this. You want to know why I didn't?"

"Because I'd've told you to shove it?"

"No," said Deakins. "I would've just killed you if you said no."

A rush of sadness came over Hale. This was Deak. *Deak*. Tears collected in his eyes.

"I was more afraid you'd say yes," Deakins said. "Because then I wouldn't be sure I could count on you."

"That's supposed to be an insult?" Hale asked.

"A fact, pal."

"That you couldn't count on me to steal nuclear weapons," Hale said. "I'm supposed to be ashamed of that?"

"No," Deakins shot back. "You should be ashamed because I couldn't count on you for anything. You don't follow up on a punch, on a girl's glance at a bar, nothing. If I had to count on you, I wouldn't've been able to see step one through."

"Well, guess what? You can count on me to stop you," Hale said. "I promise, you can count on me for that."

"I'd almost like to see it," Deakins replied. "Almost. Truth is, all this running around out here means squat. You're like one of those toy robots, all wound up and bouncing off walls. You're moving, but you haven't got a plan . . . haven't got a clue."

Hale looked at Terry, who was standing beside him, listening to the conversation. The worry in her eyes had been replaced by compassion.

"But I *do* have the nukes," Hale said. "The question is, do I also have the guts? To enter the *right* code, if you know what I mean."

Deakins was silent for a moment. "You wouldn't do that. That wouldn't be guts, pal. That'd just be saying, 'Fuck you' to me."

"Hey, that's something," Hale said. "But in case your thugs get here before I'm finished, or in case I fail, there's something I want to say to you."

"I'm all ears," said Deakins.

Hale said, "This isn't guts, man, what you're doing. This is taking a dive for bucks. After all those years of telling me how to fight, you're taking the easy way out. I may not have agreed with a lot of what you said, but I respected you.

"So, yeah," Hale said. "Fuck you, Deak. In big, shiny spades."

Hale clicked off the microphone and laid it on the tailgate. He ran his tongue over his dry lips and looked at the mine entrance.

"When was this place shut down?" he asked.

"Sometime in the 1950s," Terry said.

"How deep is it?"

"I don't know. A couple thousand feet all together, with a deck every two hundred feet or so."

Hale stared at it. He wasn't seeing the mine, but his life. Deakins was right. He didn't follow through with a lot of things.

But goddammit, he thought as he turned to the cable coiled around the winch in the front of the vehicle, *I'm going to follow through with this*.

"A couple thousand feet," he said. "Yeah, that's deep enough."

"Deep enough for what?" Terry asked.

Hale hopped off the tailgate, went around front, and pushed the Forward button. Then he picked up the cable and walked it toward the mine entrance. "A nuclear explosion," he said casually.

Terry had been walking with him. She stopped. "What?"

Upon reaching the old iron doors, Hale slipped the hook through the metal shackle at the top of the padlock, then walked back to the Humvee.

"We're going to set off the bombs," Hale said.

"You're going to set off nuclear weapons just to prove to this guy you can do it?" Terry asked. "Mister, this takes pissing contests to a whole new level."

Hale went back to the front bumper and started up the winch. "I don't have any choice." The cable lost its slack, tightened more, and both the bumper and the lock strained.

"Like hell you don't!" Terry shouted. "You can hide them!"

"Deak's got a radiation scanner. He'll find them."

Terry came around the Humvee and grabbed Hale by the shoulders. He wriggled away. "You're talking about setting off nuclear weapons!" she said.

"The military set them off underground in Nevada during the fifties and sixties," he answered. "There's no risk."

"Tell that to the giant ants," Terry said.

Though Hale was concentrating on the door, he couldn't help but smile. "I loved that picture, *Them!* And the one about the radioactive giant grasshoppers, *Beginning of the End*." He looked at her. "But those were movies, Terry. Science fiction. This is reality. We're going to be okay."

It wasn't the padlock but the hinges on the metal doors that gave way. They buckled, snapped, and then the doors flew off as though Steve Reeves had stepped behind them and given them a Herculean push. They flopped like landed marlins and Hale shut down the winch. He disconnected the hook from the padlock, which was still intact, and walked over to the mine, thinking what a shame it was that he couldn't give *Sam O. Hung Lock Company* a testimonial.

The inside was cool and damp and smelled like wet dog. But the mine's vertical shaft was right there at the entrance, which was perfect. Hale left the mine and backed the Humvee to within a yard of the entrance. Then he walked around back to the bombs.

This would be easier with two people, he thought, but he refused to ask. He spread his legs, grabbed the handles of the cocoon in which one of the weapons was resting, and pulled hard. The cradle moved, pulling the bomb an inch. He pulled again and this time there was a tearing sound. He stopped.

Hale no longer refused to ask. He looked back at Terry, who moved her hands one over the other.

"No! I am not helping you set off a nuclear weapon."

Hale let go of the handles and faced her. "We won't be down there when it goes off."

"No. He said they'd go off one minute after you set them."

"This isn't a suicide mission," Hale said. "I can do this another way."

"I said *no,*" Terry repeated. "N-O. No, no, no."

Hale shook his head. "Why am I not getting through to you?"

"Because I'm sane and you're not."

"Is that what you think?" Hale yelled. "Try this logic on for size. If we don't do this, Deakins gets the bombs back. If Deakins gets the bombs back, he holds a city for ransom. If the government doesn't pay, and it won't, my ex-partner blows the city up. And he will, trust me. What's the population of Salt Lake? Three-quarters of a million?"

"Give or take," Terry said.

"And depending on which way the wind's blowing, he gets a bonus, irradiating a large swath of Nevada and parts of California, or else Colorado and Kansas. You call me tetched for wanting to *stop* that? And then what about copycat assholes who decide to terrorize other cities? Nukes aren't as difficult to come by as you might think."

Terry exhaled forcefully. "I just can't believe he's sick enough to do it. I can't."

"Why? Because you and I wouldn't? Most people wouldn't try to shoot their flying partners in the head, or eject them without a shoulder harness. But he did. Believe me, Terry. Deak *will* nuke Salt Lake City."

Terry snarled and stalked over. She was angry—at herself, Hale figured.

"I hate these ethical dilemmas," she said. "Why can't it be like, you see someone drop a dollar and you have to decide whether or not to give it back? Why does it have to be whether to set off atomic bombs?"

"It's really the same dilemma," Hale said as she grabbed one end of a cocoon while he took the other. "It's right versus wrong. The only difference is the stakes."

"I'll say."

Hale gave her a second, then asked, "I hate to push this, but we're a little short of time. Are you ready?"

Terry took a few deep breaths, then nodded. "If we live," she said, "you can buy me dinner and tell me where this death wish of yours came from."

Hale grinned. "On three," he said.

Their faces turned red as they hoisted the weapon from the Humvee to the entrance of the mine. They laid it on the ground as gently as possible, then went back for the other. When they were finished, Hale ran back for the winch cable. He wrapped it around the fixed winglets of one, then the other, then tugged hard to test it.

"I think you should send them one at a time," Terry said.

"These things are guaranteed up to two tons," he told her. "Besides, we don't have the time."

The bombs were resting on the edge of the shaft and, to start them on their way, Hale lay on his back, braced his hands on the wall behind his head, and pushed the heads with his feet.

The weapons grated roughly against the dirt floor and swung slowly over the precipice—nose, midsection, and finally the tail. The winglets clanged against the cable as the bombs went over; the winch creaked behind them, but the cable held.

Hale rose, perspiring in little rivers. "See?" he said. "Nothing to worry about."

He ran to the front of the Humvee, got the flashlight, started the winch, then ran back. He grabbed Terry's hand on the way and pulled her toward the shaft. He sat on the edge, over the bombs.

"Sit," he said.

She did, warily, then asked why.

"Because I need you to come with me," he said as he lowered himself carefully onto the tail of one of the bombs. He stood there descending slowly, holding the cable with one hand and extending the other toward Terry. "Someone has to hold the flashlight while I set things up."

"Oh Jesus God," Terry protested, but she took his hand, climbed onto the tail of the other bomb, and rode with him into the darkness.

35

Johnson finally pinpointed the weapons using what he called his "glorified Geiger counter," a radiation detector with a sophisticated directional indicator.

"We were getting screwed up by residual uranium deposits in the hills," Johnson said as he consulted a map.

"I don't care about that," Deakins said. He was at the wheel and driving fast. "Where are they?"

"According to this," said Johnson, "they've gone to an area in the northwest, about four miles from here. There's not a hell of a lot there, just low hills and an old—"

"I know where Hale is," Deakins interrupted him and smiled. "I know where he's gone and the joke's going to be on him."

Johnson looked at Kelly, who said, "The major went over this whole area with Max. If he says he knows where Hale is, he does. And if he says there's going to be a joke on Hale, there will be."

As they rocked across the uneven ground, Deakins wanted to laugh at the irony of it all—only he couldn't laugh. Not while his nukes were in Hale's possession. Still, he wasn't unduly worried. As he thought back over the thirteen years he had known Hale, he couldn't remember a single instance of the guy being *un*predictable or having a pair that clanged or showing initiative or even following through on something he wasn't ordered to do.

There was nothing. *The guy's got no afterburners,* he told himself. What had happened today was an accident, a fluke.

Maybe he was showing off for the chick.

Pritchett was sitting in the passenger's seat, looking out the front window. There was a streak of ash along the left side of his neck, through which a stream of perspiration had cut a clean, wriggly line.

"Wait a second!" he said, turning to Deakins, "I think I've got it! Having Hale set this vehicle on fire was part of the plan all along."

Sitting behind Deakins, Kelly said, "Mr. Pritchett—"

"No, listen." He laid his hand back on the headrest. "The soot makes it harder to spot from space. And the fact that he has the nukes and we don't? No problem! He's actually got a split personality and you've cut a deal with his alter ego and—"

The rigid outside of Deakins's right hand lashed out swiftly and violently, smashing against Pritchett's Adam's apple. Pritchett's eyes went wide as eggshells and rolled toward Deakins, shocked and imploring. He gagged and clawed at his throat, and the shock turned to slitty-eyed panic as he discovered that he couldn't breathe.

Flopping around in his seat and throwing his neck against the headrest, Pritchett turned blue as he struggled to get air through his shattered windpipe. After nearly two minutes of writhing and helpless gasping, he slumped against the door. His eyes and mouth were both open. His chest wasn't moving.

Kelly said, "I, uh, thought it was bad form to kill your investors."

Deakins shrugged. "They wouldn't've let him come with us if he wasn't expendable. Like Kleenex, y'know?"

Kelly looked as if he wanted to disagree, but thought better of it.

Johnson just stared at Pritchett. "I woke up this morning never having seen a guy get killed before," Johnson said. "Now I've seen two."

Deakins said, "I woke up this morning never having killed a man before. This bunghole's one, and Hale will be number two. I mean, I dropped bombs on Baghdad." He half-smiled as his mind replayed a fond memory. "But never face-to-face." He glanced over at the gaping corpse. "Frankly, I don't know what the big deal—"

"There!" Kelly shouted as they rounded a curve.

Deakins followed his pointing finger, off to the right. There was the Humvee. *Dammit,* why had he let himself daydream like that?

He twisted the wheel, swung toward the vehicle, and saw the blasted doors and the mine entrance and the winch cable. He knew then and there that while Hale might not be overendowed in the balls department, he did have a little plan going here. And from the look of things, it was a good one.

Too bad for Hale it was not quite good enough.

36

As Hale and Terry descended, Hale used the flashlight sparingly, trying to ascertain how high above the ground they were. After a while, the air got colder and thicker, the sense of claustrophobia greater, and he kept the flashlight on just to chase away the willies. He hoped the batteries didn't run out, or they'd be screwed. Now that he thought of it, he also hoped the cable didn't run out. In his haste to get down here, it hadn't occurred to him that this section of shaft could be *deeper* than two hundred feet. The cable was two-fifty; ten of that was used up getting them over the side of the shaft, and it'd be a kick in the head if they were left dangling here. Or worse, if Deakins arrived and started winching them back up, like King Kong hauling in the vine with Fay Wray and Bruce Cabot hanging on.

Despite the cold, he was sweating freely, and it was with enormous relief that he saw the flashlight beam stop vanishing into the darkness and hit the floor of the shaft. As the bombs neared the ground, Hale handed the flashlight to Terry and jumped down. He landed right beside a horizontal crosscut. He took a moment to utter a prayer of appreciation as he stood under the bombs to ease their arrival. The irony of thanking

God for delivering weapons of mass destruction was not lost on him.

When the bombs were just a few feet up, Terry hopped down and turned the light on them. As soon as they were down, Hale unhooked the cable. He took a moment to lash it around a large boulder, sharp-edged from long-ago blasting.

"What are you doing?" she asked.

"If Deakins finds the Humvee," Hale said, "I don't want him withdrawing the cable and leaving us stranded."

"I didn't think of that," Terry said. "How long is this going to take, anyway?"

"Well," Hale said, "only a few minutes once we're in position. And we only have to set off one bomb. The other'll be buried under about a billion tons of rock. But we'll need to go deeper into the mine first."

"*What?*"

"It'll limit the amount of radiation released into the atmosphere."

"How *much* deeper?" Terry asked.

"Not very much. Let's take one down that crosscut," Hale said, "and see how far we can go."

"This is great," Terry said. She ducked into the tunnel and put the flashlight down, pointing into the crosscut, so they could see ahead. Then she ran back and helped Hale put the first bomb in. As they dragged the weapon, dirt rained down from the ceiling. "We're going to die down here. If we're not blown up, we're going to be buried in a mine cave-in. Or I'll have a heart attack."

"At least we'll be together," Hale cracked.

Terry made a point of changing the subject. "How is this going to work?" she asked.

Between pants, Hale said, "I'll use the keypad." He stopped, moved the flashlight ahead, and saw a tool nook about ten feet away. "In there," he said, pointing.

Terry stood, arched her back, and groaned.

"Nukes have two triggers," Hale said as they started up again. "Altimeter and impact. The altimeter'll set it off in the air at a certain altitude."

"Are you serious? I always thought it's supposed to hit the ground and go *boom*."

He shook his head. "Optimally, you go for the air blast. More damage that way. Three thousand feet up is the best: you get five times more destruction than at six thousand feet. Metals vaporize—"

"I get the picture," she said.

"Sorry," he said. "This is business for me. The backup trigger is impact-driven. If all else fails, the bomb'll go off when it hits the ground."

They stopped by the niche and rolled the bomb in so that the panel was facing up. Terry got the flashlight and shined it down while Hale worked the keypad.

He punched the Enter key. "There. The impact trigger is armed."

"That's it?" Terry asked, backing away.

"You expected a chirp? It's not a car alarm. And don't worry—it's not going to go off if you bump into it. It'd need to fall a good thirty or forty feet."

"Then how will you detonate it?"

"Bring the light closer, okay?"

Terry did so, with obvious reluctance, and Hale began working with the keypad.

"I'm going to reset the altimeter trigger for one hundred thousand feet. Then I'm going to tell the computer that the clock is running thirty minutes fast. When thirty minutes are up, the system will reboot, the altimeter will read that the bomb's below one hundred thousand feet, and . . . well, boom. Understand?"

"Not in the least," Terry said.

Hale finished entering the new program, then he stood. "It means that as soon as I enter the numbers into the clock, we're going to have thirty minutes to get clear of here. If not, we'll be indistinguishable from coal dust."

"Got it," Terry said. "So what are you waiting for?"

Hale said, "Just running down a mental checklist to make sure I didn't forget anything."

"But *do* you know what you're doing? I mean, we *will* have thirty minutes to get clear?"

Hale said, "Pilots who fly with nuclear weapons have to know these babies. If something like this happens, we've got standing orders, and I quote, 'To retrieve if possible, disable if necessary, and destroy if we must.' And destroy I must. Now, I just have to set the clock and—"

Suddenly, the glowing numbers of the ECU clock flickered, the readout went blank, and Hale stood staring at it as if he had just been told he was getting into the ring with Mike Tyson. . . .

37

The crisis management team was back in the Situation Room, reviewing the psych profiles of Hale and Deakins, when the phone rang beside General Creeley. He answered it, listened, and then hung up. All he'd said was "Hello" and "Send them through at half-minute intervals."

"We've got the pictures," he said as the wide-view bird's-eye, thermal image of rocky terrain from the National Reconnaissance Office filled the computer screens.

Conversation about how quiet and secretive Hale seemed, and how gregarious and outgoing Deakins was, was tabled as Creeley rose.

"This is the KH-12 satellite's infrared view of the crash site," he said. "Now, an exposed nuclear core would be relatively hot, of course. It'd show here as a circle of bright white. As you can see, there's nothing."

He waited for the second picture to pop on, as if this were a slide show. It was another bird's-eye view, this one with four dull red blotches.

"The only heat signatures we found were these," he said. He raised his eyes from the screen and looked slowly around the table. "We think it's Colonel Rhodes and his men. Their bodies. Living targets are brighter."

Chairman Dryfoos and Baird exchanged looks. Baird nodded. The chairman reached for the phone.

"Get me Colonel Wilkins," he said.

Not a word was spoken as he waited. Baird was thinking about this sullen Captain Hale. How the hell had a guy like that been handed a bomber and a pair of nuclear missiles? What if he hadn't decided to play games, but had gone right to Washington or New York or Los Angeles and decided to lay his eggs there?

"Colonel," Dryfoos said, putting the call on Speaker when Wilkins came on. "It looks like we've been caught with our pants down. Colonel Rhodes and his party are dead, and not only aren't the bombs hot, they aren't anywhere to be found. We're going to need an S&D squadron out there. Fast."

"I've got ten ships equipped with radiation sensors ready to go," Wilkins said. "NEST is out of the plane and in the chopper, and they'll be on the scene in less than an hour."

"Good," Dryfoos said. "Tell your team that I want the pilots of the B-3 brought back here if possible. Tell them I want that very, very much."

"Yes, sir," Wilkins said, and hung up.

Baird looked at Dryfoos. "I'm going to have my people make sure there aren't any reporters sniffing around this yet," he said. "That isn't how we want the President to find out."

Dryfoos nodded.

"If not, I'd still rather not wake him. Especially knowing as little as we do about this damn thing."

"Right," said Dryfoos. He turned to Creeley and Schneider. "You gentlemen better change the flight assignments of your other pilots, just in case there's more than one crew involved in this."

Both agreed.

Baird looked at the last photograph, which was still on the screen. Hale—or whoever—had not hesitated to kill four people. As horrible as that was, he knew it was nothing compared to what he might be facing before this day was through.

38

"Shit!" Hale said. "Shit, shit, shit."

Terry ventured closer. "What's wrong?"

Hale gestured toward the bomb. "The clock's dead. The electronics must've been damaged in the fall."

Hale went to kick the bomb, turned at the last moment, and kicked the wall. Terry breathed easier.

Hale looked back at the bomb. "I need the clock to set off the nuke. Goddamn it. *Shit!*"

"There's no other way?" Terry asked. "Something like this—it's got to have backups."

"Oh, yeah, it surely does. I could set it off manually, but I'd really rather not do that."

"Then I guess we have no choice. We have to go back to the shaft and get the other nuke."

Hale took the flashlight from her and shined it around the tunnel. "There really isn't time for that. Freakin' Deak'll be breathing down our hot little necks soon."

He shined the light on the ceiling and on the walls. Eyebolts had been screwed into the cross beams. He lingered on them for a moment.

"Maybe there's another way," he said.

"Like what?"

Hale looked at her. "I'm gonna need your belt and one of your socks."

She looked pained. "My belt and—"

"A sock," Hale said. "And quickly."

Reluctantly, wondering how much more of this crap she could possibly take, Terry undid her buckle and whipped off her belt, then removed a shoe.

"Why couldn't we use one of yours?" she grumbled as she ripped open the laces and tugged off the sock.

"Because mine have holes in them," he said as he took the sock, squatted on the floor, and began filling it with sand.

39

Deakins stood by the mine entrance, sucking on his upper lip, feeling the satisfying, very compact weight of the Uzi in his right hand. Several paces closer to the mine stood Kelly, with a semiautomatic slung across his back, a bandanna tied around his forehead, and a flashlight poked through a loop in his belt.

As he waited for the fastidious James Johnson to finish checking the Humvee winch for booby traps, Deakins tried hard to decide whether he was giving Hale way too much credit.

Question, Deakins said to himself. *Could Hale have rigged the bombs to fall if I try to winch them up? Are the bombs somewhere else? Or is the jerk just hanging in the darkness, waiting to shoot whoever shows his face?*

Deakins's eyes rose from the shattered doors to Kelly, who stood like a chess piece waiting for the grand master's hand. A large part of Deakins wanted to be the first one down, but he held back—not because of cowardice, but because if Hale were waiting, he didn't want to give him the satisfaction of killing him.

Johnson told Deakins that the winch was okay.

"Go," Deakins said to Kelly. "Just remember one thing."

Kelly looked at him.

"There's a thermonuclear warhead down there," Deakins said. "Try not to shoot it."

Kelly saluted with the barrel of his weapon, then strode purposefully to the mine entrance. He flicked on the flashlight, studied the shaft for a moment, then began to rappel down.

Deakins was oblivious to the heat of the sun and to the few insects that were drawn to his sweat. After nearly a minute, he walked toward the mine, and had to stop himself from going down. He wanted Hale *now*. He wanted him bent over a cannon and taking a cat-o'-nine-tails across his bare back. Or keel-hauled. Or dispatched with a few blows to the temple or even a shot in the forehead. Anything.

Johnson walked over to their Humvee and pulled on a black canvas backpack with a suitcase inside. He secured the snaps then leaned against the side of the car, arms folded.

Finally, Kelly yelled, "All clear!" He added, "One of the nukes is here, and it looks okay."

Deakins motioned briskly for Johnson to go ahead, then ran forward himself.

Is the bomb bait, or did Hale run out of time? Deakins wondered. The latter, he told himself. It had to be. Hale wouldn't have had the time to do anything clever or fancy.

When he reached the bottom, Deakins found Kelly squatting beside the weapon. The panel was off, the controls exposed.

"He didn't screw around with it," Kelly said. "You want to send it up?"

Deakins shook his head. He picked up the flashlight, looked around the dark shaft, felt the damp, brittle rock.

"I believe I know what the little pecker is planning." He smiled. "Thing is, he's got to get out of here before he does it. And that may prove difficult."

Deakins shined the light down the crosscut. He saw the footprints and drag marks in the damp dirt.

"Come on," he said to the others. "Let's go find the other weapon first."

40

"I don't remember this . . . being in my . . . job description."

Terry was breathing heavily as Hale sat on top of her shoulders. He had filled her sock with sand and pushed the open end through one of the eyebolts in the cross beam. Now he was tightening her belt around the open end.

"Okay," Hale said.

Hale held onto the crossbeam with one hand and handed Terry the free end of the belt. She moved out from beneath him and he released the beam and dropped lightly to the ground. She gave the belt back to him.

"Thanks," he said. "Let me have one of those rocks." He pointed to a small pile lying against a wall.

Terry gave him the rock and he looped the end of the belt around it. Then he let go: the rock was now suspended from the belt, hanging above the bomb, over the open panel. The sand prevented the sock from going through the hole in the crossbeam, which kept the rock from dropping.

Hale knelt beside the panel. He had used the tongue of Terry's belt buckle to pry up the clock, exposing a circuit board beneath. Now, using his fingernails, he pulled a stamp-sized chip from the board without breaking the two thin wires attached to it. He looked up, and moved the chip so that it was directly beneath the rock.

"I just want you to know," Terry said, "that I trust you—but I don't have a clue as to what you're planning."

"Ever hear of Mousetrap?" Hale asked as he reached to the side, picked up a small rock, and laid it on top of the chip.

"The play?" Terry asked.

"No," said Hale. "The game."

She shook her head. "Like I said, we move in different cultural circles."

Hale said, "It's a game where one object hits another object which hits another until the cage falls on the little mouse."

"Oh," she said. "Like a Rube Goldberg cartoon."

"You got it," said Hale. "Our Mousetrap is, we cut a hole in the sock, and when enough sand drains out—and we're hopefully in New Mexico somewhere—the sock is pulled through the eyebolt, the rock drops, hitting the rock on this chip, closing the firing circuit and that's it."

Hale stood and checked the alignment once more.

"How much time are we going to have?" Terry asked.

"I don't know precisely," Hale said. "This isn't a Swiss sock. Twenty minutes, maybe. I didn't want to give it so much time that Deakins could—"

Hale was cut off as a pair of bullets flew in, ricocheting off the uneven rock walls.

"Down!" Hale screamed, pushing her to the ground beside the bomb and falling on top of her.

He craned around and looked back along the crosscut. A second pair of muzzle flashes lit Kelly's face.

"Shit," Hale whispered. "It's them already."

"I figured," Terry said.

"Can you reach the flashlight and shut it?"

"Yes," she said. "Do you hear a hissing?" she asked.

Hale said he didn't, and as Terry stretched an arm ahead, Hale reached down to his belt and pulled out the gun he'd taken from Baker. He remained on top of her, and as he shifted his position slightly to return fire, he felt a tickling on his cheek.

"Uh-oh," Terry said, pointing the beam up.

Hale followed the shaft of light, saw the line of dark sand falling toward him.

"Aw, Christ," he said, and half-rising, he reached for the belt.

A bullet whizzed by Hale's hand, grazing it. He yowled and quickly withdrew it.

"Got a problem?" Deakins laughed from somewhere behind them.

"We *all* do, asshole!" Hale yelled. "You think you're safe there?"

"No. But y'know, ever since I saw *Rebel Without a Cause* I've wanted to play a serious game of chicken. You up for it, buddy?"

Terry squirmed out from under Hale. "I saw that movie on laser disc," she said. "Deakins can be James Dean if he wants to—we're bailing out."

She shined the flashlight down the tunnel and grabbed Hale's wounded hand. He screamed.

"Sorry," she said, and quickly took his other hand. "Come on!"

"Where?" Hale said.

Terry pulled hard and he followed her down the crosscut. "Remember why I told you they closed this mine?"

"A river or something," he said.

"Right. That may be our way out."

"But we can't outrun a bomb!" Hale said.

"Why not? We were going to before."

"Yeah, when I was gonna punch a pinhole," Hale said. "The sock is draining way too fast."

She stopped. "So we don't have twenty minutes?"

"We may have a quarter of that," Hale said. "You find the way out and run. I'll shut the thing down and try to get Deakins."

"You're gonna get killed and they'll have two nuclear weapons."

"Once again, I don't have any choice," Hale said.

"Maybe not, but I'm coming with—"

"No!" Hale yelled and started back in the dark. "I don't want that on my conscience."

"You'll be dead. You won't know." She held her gun and the flashlight at her side. "You want to argue, or you want to go back and try to frag Deakins? We're running out of time."

Hale took her in with his eyes. "You sure you're a park ranger and not a U.S. Army Ranger?" he asked as they ran back along the tunnel.

"Right now," she said, "I'm only sure of one thing: we're both very insane."

Hale wasn't about to argue, especially as they reached the bomb just when Deakins and his men arrived from the other side.

41

Gunfire pushed Hale and Terry back into the dark, but not before Hale saw the sock run out of sand just as Deakins arrived; Deakins snatched the rock from the air as it fell.

James Dean my ass, he thought as Deakins tossed the rock aside and looked down at the bomb.

Another of Kelly's shells zipped by Hale, and he told Terry to douse her flashlight. He pressed his back to the wall of the shaft, Terry close beside him on the right. Hale no longer had a clear sight line to Deakins and his team.

"Very impressive," Deakins called out, his voice echoing down the tunnel. "I do think this little chain reaction would have socked it to me, partner."

Hale heard the crunch of footsteps in the dirt, coming toward them. He wondered what Deakins was planning. He wouldn't risk throwing grenades down here: the explosion would bring the mine down around them. But he was up to something. Deakins was always working an angle.

"That was smart, turning off your light," Deakins continued. "Maybe I won't be able to find you. One trouble with that, though—"

Hale heard a distinctive *click,* the sound of a switch being flipped. He flinched, then raised his automatic as a string of recessed lights went on at their feet.

The lights illuminated Hale, Terry, and Deakins, who was standing at the mouth of the crosscut, his Uzi held hip-high. Hale and Deakins faced each other for a moment, their eyes locked, weapons pointed at each other. Then Deakins squeezed the trigger, peppering the tunnel with a short burst.

Hale pushed Terry back the way they'd come, firing his automatic behind him as he followed her.

"You want to know what's sort of funny?" Deakins shouted as he followed them into the crosscut. "You did me a favor. See, Hale—you aren't the only one who's thought of setting off a nuke in this mine."

No, Hale thought as he ran. *That's bullshit.* Deakins was just making a show for his men, the old "I meant to do that" drill.

But when he heard the rest of what Deakins had to say, Hale felt the same hurling sensation he used to get during G-force tests his rookie year.

"I need a demonstration," Deakins said as he chased Hale further with another burst. "Otherwise, some swinging dick in Washington is going to say I don't have the *cajones* or the ability to set off a nuke. I think it's important I show them that I'm ready, willing, and able. Hell, I'm *eager.* Of course, I won't leave the other nuke down here like you were going to do. You can see why that wouldn't work for me."

Hale was tempted to turn around and go man-to-man with the bastard, but he kept running. A showdown wouldn't accomplish much: Terry would stop running, too, and Deakins's flunkies would continue the operation anyway. It was more important to get out and get help.

There were two gunshots from the vertical shaft. Deakins's footsteps stopped.

"That's my cue to leave," he yelled. "My lads have finished inputting the code—the correct code, Hale—so I hope you enjoy these last minutes of life. Oh, and Hale? Just so you know, if you try to remove the external timer we've attached to the bomb, you won't have to worry about 'going to the light,' as they say. The light will most definitely come to you."

Hale stopped running as Deakins's footsteps echoed faintly and then were gone. The tunnel was still and close and he could hear his own heartbeat.

Terry shined the light on his face.

"That's an 'I've got to go back' look if I've ever seen one."

Hale said, "He has to have left himself time to haul the other nuke up. That'll give *me* time to get back there."

"To do what?"

He started back along the tunnel. "Try to shut the damn thing down."

42

Deakins found it fitting that all those years of punching the crap out of Hale had left his arm strong enough to climb the Humvee cable.

He had told Johnson and Kelly to wait in the shaft and help guide the nuke back up. Upon reaching the Humvee, Deakins started the winch on its way up. While it pulled the bomb back to the surface, he went to the burned Humvee and moved it beside the other. When the bomb had reached the bottom of the winch, Deakins punched the Stop button, unhooked the cable, and sent it back down the mine shaft.

After nearly a minute, one of the men fired a shot. Deakins stopped the winch. When a second shot was fired, the colonel started winding the cable in. After hoisting the bomb into the Humvee—again crediting Hale for having helped to pump him up—he walked away from the Humvee, bent slightly toward the horizon, and listened.

Almost at once, he heard the *whump, whump, whump*.

The NEST boys are a little early, he thought, *but I can deal with that.*

Loping back to the winch, Deakins casually pressed the Stop button.

"*Hey!*" Kelly shouted from the mine. "What's up?"

Deakins stepped over the cable, opened the Humvee door, leaned in, and shifted the vehicle into Neutral. Then he popped the parking brake.

"Major!" Kelly yelled. "We're goin' back down!"

"Hang on!" Deakins laughed as the truck edged toward the mine entrance, pulled by the weight of Kelly and Johnson.

"*What are you doing?*" Kelly screamed as the vehicle picked up speed.

"Getting ready to leave," Deakins said under his breath as he climbed into his Humvee, started the engine, and reset the trip odometer to zero.

As he sped away, Deakins watched in his rearview mirror as the other Humvee clanked over the fallen doors. It hopped and landed slightly off-course, the driver's side front fender scraping the mine entrance.

"Shit," Deakins scowled, and touched the brake.

But the vehicle caromed off the support beam and raced through the entrance as planned. The front wheels shot over the edge of the vertical shaft, and then the long, heavy undercarriage scraped the edge of the pit. That provided enough drag to stop the vehicle, which hung there for an everlasting moment, teetering precipitously, threatening not to fall.

Deakins pressed the brake harder and was prepared to go back and give the Humvee a shove when the front-heavy truck suddenly tumbled into the shaft. There were screams and loud banging as it fell, followed by a horrible, grinding crash—and then silence.

Smiling, Deakins pushed down on the gas pedal. He unhooked a small, black box from his belt, then winked at the figure in the passenger's seat.

"We're going to be fine," Deakins said. "I told you there was nothing to worry about."

Yet he imagined that even if Pritchett were alive, the ripening little tenderfoot would have found something else to complain about. . . .

43

Moments before the crash of the Humvee, Hale was crouched beside the bomb, punching keys on the timer control. His eyes stung from sweat and his hair was matted and cold.

Against his wishes, Terry had joined him; there'd been no time to argue and, he had to admit, if he didn't pull this off, chances were good she'd collect six hundred to eight hundred rads and be dead within two years anyway. Here, at least, there would be total, instantaneous destruction.

"Try his birthday," she suggested.

Hale punched in the numbers. "No good."

"Maybe he's got a sick sense of humor. Try your birthday."

Hale did. "Nothing. Goddammit, *nothing works*!"

"Try his dog's birthday . . . his Social Security number . . . the fastest speed he's ever flown."

"I don't know any of that shit!" Hale said, rattling his fists with exasperation. The external timer was tucked in a backpack beside the bomb, and the white numbers read two minutes, three seconds. Hale wished that he knew more about these things. He wished that instead of boxing, he'd taken some of the courses the Air Force had offered—

Hale fired a look at Terry, then picked up his gun. "Terry, we're out of options. I've gotta use this."

"Shoot the bomb?" she said, staring at the automatic. "If you do, won't that—"

"Yeah," Hale said. "But *we* can't get out, and if we blow this now it might take Deakins with us."

"Might?"

Hale shrugged. "He could be clear by now."

"But there's a chance—"

Hale nodded.

"Then do it," she said. "Do it, quickly."

Hale turned purposefully toward the timer. "Stand back. The bullets may bounce."

"Like that matters?" Terry asked.

Hale said, "You've got a point."

"We'll stand together," Terry said bravely. She knelt beside him and put her arms around his shoulders, her hands on his chest.

Hale thought, *What a piece of work is man.* Here he was, moments from judgment at the Pearly Gates, and all he could think about was how her touch thrilled him right down to his knees.

He was about to fire the gun when they heard the crash and looked down the lighted shaft and saw clouds of dirt rolling toward them through the crosscut.

"What the hell?" Hale said, rising.

"It must have been an explosion," Terry said.

"No," said Hale. "We'd be deaf if it were."

He started running toward the main shaft, breathing through a handkerchief. Terry ran after him, coughing.

Rocks were still tumbling down, and when they reached the vertical shaft, only a few spears of daylight pierced the piled debris. But it was enough to illuminate the smashed Humvee and the broken body of Kelly, who lay bent in half, the back of his head to his feet, beneath the front of the vehicle.

"The co . . . co . . . ." said a voice to the corner.

Hale turned to his left. He saw a bloodied figure lying well away from the Humvee; dust was already settling on his wounds, making them look even uglier.

"That's one of Deak's men," Terry said. "He must have jumped free."

James Johnson shuddered violently as he tried to rise on an elbow. "I know . . . the code . . . ," he gasped.

"You know?" Hale bent beside the shattered man. "What is it? Quickly!"

"Take . . . me," he said. "*I* want . . . to do it. The back-stabbing . . . mother. . . ."

There was no time to argue. Swearing and scooping the man onto his shoulder, Hale ran through the crosscut, hoping the poor broken bastard didn't die before they got there.

When they reached the bomb, Hale set Johnson down beside it and looked into his face. His eyes were shut, but he was still breathing.

So was Hale—hard. There were eighteen seconds left on the timer.

Kneeling beside the man and cradling him in his arms, Hale took his hand and put it on the keypad. He stretched out the man's index finger, which was lit by the amber glow of the Active light.

Hale leaned close to his ear. "Start pushing," he said. "Fast."

Johnson smiled and opened his eyes. He pressed zero, seven, two, nine, seven, seven.

"The . . . only lottery number . . . he ever won," the man explained, then hit Enter. The clock stopped at 002 and the red Deactivated light came on; the amber light winked off, as dead as the green Detonate light.

Terry laughed a nervous laugh. "I knew the code would be something infantile."

Hale used the dusty handkerchief to wipe his mouth and

brow. He looked into Johnson's eyes; set in that dirty face, they were misleadingly bright.

"Thanks," Hale said. "What happened?"

Johnson winced as he tried to lie back. Hale helped him.

"Deak . . . was pulling us up . . . let the truck . . . roll in."

"He gets his kicks in funny ways," Hale said. "You gotta watch that."

Johnson nodded. "I shoulda known . . . when he killed Pritchett. I shoulda known. . . ."

"Is there anything you can tell us about his plan?" Hale asked.

Johnson shook his head. "Everything was . . . a need-to-know basis."

"I understand," Hale said as he wiped some of the grime off Johnson's face. There was blood on his lips and he touched the handkerchief to them. "Look, we're going to go. But as soon as we get out, I'll send help. I'm sorry I don't have water or anything to leave you—"

"'S'okay," Johnson said. "Just leave me . . . to contemplate . . . my sins."

Hale patted him on the cheek and rose. "You atoned for them. Just sit tight, okay?"

"Okay," Johnson said. "Just one thing, though."

Hale looked down at him benignly. "What's that?"

"Hurry." Johnson cocked a thumb toward the backpack. "That's more than . . . just . . . a timer."

Hale felt sick again. "What is it?"

"A . . . remote. When Deak's outta range, if it hasn't blown . . . he can blow it."

"Ohmigod," Terry said.

Hale bent to pick Johnson up. "Come on—"

"No, man," Johnson said. "I'm drinkin' . . . my own heart blood here. Just leave me."

"I won't—"

"You will." Johnson slipped his automatic from its holster, aimed it at Terry. "Ain't that I love ya . . . but you're the only ones . . . who can kick his . . . nuts."

"Let's go," Terry said, tugging Hale's arm.

Reluctantly, Hale backed off.

"You hear?" Johnson said. "I want 'em kicked . . . bad."

"I hear," Hale said as they started down the tunnel. They were moving away from the main shaft.

The lights stopped as they entered areas that had never been wired, and soon Hale and Terry were once again running by the fading, yellow glow of the flashlight. She was a pace ahead of him. Both of them wheezed as the air thinned.

"Would you mind telling me how far away this river of yours is?" Hale asked.

"I'm not sure," she admitted.

"Are we talking yards or miles?"

"I don't know!" she said. "Now, be quiet. I'm listening."

Hale shut up, though he kept his mouth open to suck down air. His legs ached, especially around the thighs. He was a pilot, not a runner. He was accustomed to sitting on his butt in a nice, comfortable seat, not running marathons.

Then he felt a faint rumbling, the cavern floor vibrating like the seats at a rock concert. And he heard what sounded like blood rushing through his ears, only it wasn't blood. Finally, they came to another vertical shaft. As they stood beside it, the roar was nearly deafening.

Terry was breathing heavily. "This is it!" she yelled. "The underground river."

Hale peered into the darkness. "How far down is it?"

"I don't know," Terry admitted.

"Where does it go?"

"I don't know that either," she said. "It could honeycomb the substrata for miles, or it could end in an underground lake somewhere."

"I've heard about those," Hale said. "They're dark and still and there may even be dinosaurs down there because the lakes haven't seen daylight since one million B.C."

Terry nodded. "It could be dangerous. Would you rather go back and try to dig our way out of the mine shaft?"

Hale said, "I'm for facing the dinos."

Terry tucked her flashlight into her belt and smiled. "Me, too. I suggest we hold hands so we don't get separated."

Hale agreed. Holding his automatic tightly in his left hand, he folded her slender fingers in his right. He felt the thrill again, and wondered if she were experiencing a similar excitement—or if that sweaty palm of hers was just plain terror.

"Count of three?" he said, smiling in spite of everything. He felt good that they'd managed to survive since the last time they'd heard those words.

"On three, Sundance," she agreed. "One . . . two . . . *three!*"

They leaped together, but their hands came apart the instant they struck the icy, churning water. Hale was totally disoriented as the turbulent river swept him through the blackest black he'd ever experienced, the current pulling him under and then popping him back up, wavelets sloshing down his throat and making it impossible for him to call Terry. He moaned as something hard and sharp thudded against his temple, then again as another knife-like object struck the back of his head. And suddenly it was a struggle to stay afloat and awake, and he gurgled as he fell face-forward. . . .

44

Deakins vowed never again to take rearview mirrors for granted. First with the Humvee and its ass-over-teakettle trip down the shaft, and now with the NEST chopper, it was a real friend, a true ally in the Cause.

So was the oft-ignored odometer. He watched as it clicked over from 2.9 to 3 miles, put an extra half mile between himself and the mine, then waited. He looked at his watch.

Eleven minutes, three seconds. The bomb was late.

"It appears that Hale may've figured out the code," Deakins said to Pritchett as he climbed from the Humvee. "It's a googolplex-to-one shot, but hey—they happen."

He hoped they did, anyway. He hoped that Johnson hadn't screwed up attaching the external timer.

The shmuck, he thought.

Deakins was glad he'd wasted Johnson and Kelly: he'd known that they and Baker were losers when he'd first contacted them through the classifieds in *Weekend Muster* magazine. They'd done their jobs, and Deakins was sorry he'd never recover the money he'd paid them, but then that was the price of doing business. Sometimes, you had to pay guys before you killed them.

He unhooked the black box from his belt, flipped the cap, and pressed a white button. A black button popped up beside it, he put his thumb on it, and he waited.

The NEST chopper was about a quarter mile away, three hundred feet up, and coming in over the hills. He smiled, started to hum "Oh, What a Beautiful Morning," and watched the Army's danger guys approach. He could picture them in the Jetranger cabin, all rah-rah confidence in their black radiation suits. Six NEST eggs and a mother hen and one big, collective hard-on for him.

A line of bullets kicked up dust on both sides of the Humvee. Deakins didn't budge as they chewed up dirt near his feet.

"Letting me know that you mean business?" Deakins said. "*Oh,* what a hard-on."

He watched, across the flat plain, as the chopper descended and swept into the gap between the hills, flying toward the mine entrance.

A loud crackling spilled from the sky as the helicopter loudspeaker came on.

"*Do not move or you'll be fired on!*"

Deakins recognized the manly, mechanical voice as belonging to Colonel "Fox" Hunt.

"In just a few moments you'll be able to compare notes with your esteemed ancestor," Deakins said to himself as he watched the chopper.

When the Jetranger was lower and in front of the mine, Deakins pushed the button.

Johnson hadn't screwed up.

An atomic bomb begins as a bluish-white blast which heats the surrounding air to eighteen million degrees Fahrenheit—more than half the temperature of the core of the sun. It creates a fireball whose radiant heat travels at the speed of light, and causes a pressure wave that moves at 1,150 feet each second. In the air, the overpressure of the blast wave creates negative pressure which sucks winds in excess of six hundred miles and hour into the ravaged area; as the fireball rises, it draws these winds and debris with it, generating the familiar mushroom cloud.

There is no mushroom cloud underground, though the heat is sufficient to turn rock to gas, and the pressure wave is equivalent to the epicenter of a magnitude nine earthquake. And the sound—

The roar was everywhere, and Deakins felt like a tic on a drum in the opening measures of *Also Sprach Zarathustra*. His ears ached as if he'd been punched hard on both sides, and he saw the mouth of the mine spit dirt and light and the ground ripple toward him, like the windblown surface of a lake. When it reached him, he was hurled, along with the Humvee, nearly three feet in the air.

But not before he saw the shock wave hit the chopper. The blast threw the Jetranger tail rotor over the flight deck, simultaneously killing every piece of electronic equipment in the aircraft. Shock-blown and out of control, it was thrown against a rock spire west of the mine and vanished in a flash of fire. The explosion of the chopper seemed—*was*—pitiful compared to the complete sensory overload of the atom blast.

Deakins landed on his backside, the resilient Humvee on its wheels.

He sat there and watched, as if they were July Fourth fireworks, the chopper and its go-get-'em crew burn amid the scrub, and the main entrance belch out the last of its smoke and nova-white fire.

Slapping his knees and rising, Deakins brushed himself off as he walked to the Humvee. He leaned in the open window.

"At least I know they work," he said to the ambivalent corpse.

Deakins stepped back, stretched, slapped the sturdy vehicle

on the roof, then climbed in. He started up the Humvee and then leaned to the right, toward Pritchett.

"You see, Mr. Pritchett? As I've said from the start, there really is nothing to worry about. Not unless you're the U.S. government, because right about now they should be crapping melons over at McMurran."

45

The hanging fluorescent lamps swung and pictures fell in the control room at McMurran. Wilkins looked across the desk at Giles, who was no longer rosy-cheeked as he twisted slowly on his swivel chair, spun by the blast. The baby-faced Washingtonian planted his feet on the floor to stop the chair from turning.

The shaking lasted just over fifteen seconds, and was followed by an eerie stillness. Barking dogs and chirping birds, who had not been expecting a tremor, were silent. Alarms had gone off around the base, and were quickly shut down. No one was shouting: people were always quiet and alert in the aftermath of temblors.

Giles chuckled anxiously. "That's all we need. A goddamn earthquake and aftershocks."

A picture of Wilkins's wife and children had fallen flat on the desk. He picked up the photograph, and then he picked up the phone.

"Son," Wilkins said, "I was at the Nevada Test Site in the fifties. That wasn't an earthquake."

"No?" Giles said, clearly on the verge of freaking. "*No?*"

Wilkins said into the phone, "Get me the Room." Then he said to Giles, "No. That was a nuclear explosion."

Giles jumped up and headed for the door. "That's it. I'm out of here."

"Relax," Wilkins said, "you're going to be fine. That was an underground blast. No radiation to speak of."

"Huh?" Giles stopped. "How do you know?"

"For one thing, if it were aboveground it wouldn't have caused the same kind of rumbling ground tremor we felt. For another, if it were aboveground, we'd all be blind, melting, and dying." Wilkins said into the phone, "Hello. This is Colonel Wilkins for General Creeley."

A moment later Creeley came on and told him he was on the speaker phone.

"General Creeley," Wilkins said, "gentlemen, it's happened. We've just had a detonation."

"Christ Jesus," Creeley said. "What kind?"

"Underground," Wilkins said. "I'm sure of it. If I had to guess, I'd say our NEST guys found the bombs, couldn't absolutely secure them, and set them off in a cave or mine to render them useless. We've used that scenario in our terrorist exercise simulations."

"But this is speculation," Creeley said. "You have no first-hand knowledge."

"None," Wilkins admitted. "And we may not have for some time."

"Why?" asked Chief of Staff Baird.

"NEST may not have wanted to communicate with us for fear of tipping off Hale or whoever was looking for the bombs," Wilkins said. "Afterward, they wouldn't have been able to communicate with us because of the EMP."

"EMP?" said Baird.

"Electromagnetic pulse," Wilkins explained. "It's released in a nuclear detonation, and it wipes out anything electronic for miles. The EMP is going to hurt us as well, because it'll disable *all* radio communications in the vicinity for the next few hours."

"Any chance that the NEST team was not the perpetrator of this explosion?" Dryfoos asked.

"Of course that's possible," said Wilkins. "The hijacker may have encountered NEST and set the bomb off to keep from being apprehended."

"Helluva smoke screen," Schneider laughed.

"Just to make sure we consider every option," Dryfoos continued, "could NEST also have been a victim of the blast?"

"If their Jetranger was within three or four miles of the blast," Wilkins said, "on the ground or airborne, it's conceivable the shock wave could have gotten them. Yes, sir. They could be victims."

There was a short silence, and then Baird said, "Colonel— tell my associate Giles that I have a lot of faith in him. But in spite of his belief that honesty is the best policy, I want a huge lid on this goddamn thing. Got that?"

Wilkins's eyes rose to Giles, who was still shaking even though the ground was not. "Yes."

Baird said, "From now on and until the end of time, what happened in Utah today was an earthquake. All right?"

"All right."

"We're going to have to work on the seismographic facilities," Creeley said, "tell them to go along with the earthquake story."

"They won't," said Baird. "Scientists aren't like the rest of us. They know a lot but don't understand a thing."

"They understand the words 'government subsidy,'" Schneider said. "They'll play ball."

"I hope you're right," Baird said.

Wilkins was suddenly anxious to end the conversation. It wasn't just because he was getting bored with the horseshit, cover-up side of it, but because he was getting nervous. Despite his off-the-cuff analysis, he knew the NEST team *could* have sent word, in code, of their plans. Colonel Hunt was a pretty conservative soldier: if he were going to fire up a nuclear bomb, he would've tried to let someone know.

But what if that wasn't what happened at all? he thought. The hijacking was obviously well planned. What if it were even more well planned than anyone but Giles seemed to think?

Wilkins said, "We'll contact you if we learn anything else."

Now Giles piped up. "Colonel? Would you please inform them that *I* believe they'll get something before we do."

Wilkins looked at him. "Such as?"

"A ransom demand," Giles said. "I think this explosion bears out my hypothesis. It was a wake-up call. If I'm correct, it was just one bomb that went off. The second blast will come soon, and I assure you it will not be underground . . . and it definitely will not be in a national park."

46

Terry knew at once that they were in trouble.

She wasn't surprised that she'd lost her companion. Just jumping into a pool holding hands had never been easy. A person's instinct is to pull in their arms when they hit the water, to protect their sides from the cold. She'd tried to grab Hale again when they were separated, but the darkness and madly twisting current made that impossible.

Then there were the stalactites.

Moments after she hit the water, Terry felt a jagged rock scrape the top of her head. She went underwater to try and avoid them and realized the captain might not think to do that. A few clunks on the head and he might already be unconscious. Snatching her flashlight from her belt, she paddled to the surface, thrust her face up, and swept the beam across the torrent.

Almost at once, she had to duck under to avoid a saber-sharp stalactite.

She gasped, surfacing, and looked around: the jagged cones were everywhere, like icicles under a sundeck.

Then she saw the captain ahead and to the left. He was turning over and over, his mouth open, his eyes barely so.

There was a gash on his forehead, and each time he went under the blood washed over his face.

With another oath, Terry dove underwater and swam toward him. She followed the rippling white beam through the clear water, then grabbed Hale by his flight suit collar.

"Are you all right?" she screamed.

He nodded faintly, and she pulled him under as they were carried past another row of stalactites.

Before Terry could hoist Hale up again, they were carried down a short waterfall and buffeted by the eddies at its base. When she and Hale were finally spun free, Terry managed to raise her waterlogged arm and shine the flashlight ahead. Though there were no longer any stalactites, the roof of the cavern was getting lower; the water was also no longer spring clear, but brownish.

"Take a breath," she said. "You're going to need it."

Hale did, and once again Terry took him underwater. She dropped the flashlight so she could use her right hand to paddle. Kicking forward, her legs straining, her arm cramping around Hale, she swam through the murk. It was strange how when the bomb was about to explode, she hadn't really believed she was about to die. After all, she'd felt perfectly fine then.

This was different. Her head was pounding, her lungs demanded air, and her limbs felt like wet sand. And there was the added terror of the dark and not knowing when the channel would end. Or if it would end. They could very well join the trilobites and other fossilized sea life down here, destined for a museum display in some future millennium. Or worse, a museum gift shop.

But the darkness quickly gave way to brown light and then amber light and soon it was all white and blue above them. Kicking furiously, Terry broke the surface of the Colorado

River and pulled down the sweetest lungsful of air she had ever tasted.

Her companion did not. With an oath, Terry swam toward shore, dragging Hale. When they reached the rocky edge of the river, she threw him down, turned his head to the side to fish out anything he might have swallowed in the water, then pinched his nose shut with her finger and thumb. Bending over him, Terry put her mouth to his and delivered two quick, full breaths. She checked his pulse. It was there, steady, but he didn't breathe.

"C'mon, you," she said. She replaced her mouth and gave him a breath, sat back and counted to five-one-thousand while she waited for him to breathe; gave him another, and repeated. "You're a bird, and no one expects you to swim," she said, sitting back. "But you *can* breathe, can't you?"

After ten breaths, Terry was rewarded with a gasp and a shudder from Hale. His eyes opened and he looked past her, then at her.

"That wasn't at all like *Pirates of the Caribbean*," he observed.

"No, it wasn't." She reached into her pocket, took out a packet of soaked Kleenex, and lay the wet tissues on his gashed forehead. "How much do you remember?"

Hale tried to get up but didn't make it. He fell back, shut his eyes. "I remember feeling like a pachinko ball getting bounced between the pegs."

"That's just about what you were," Terry said. "One thing, though. How'd you manage to hold onto that?"

She dipped her forehead to Hale's left hand. He was still gripping the automatic he'd taken from Baker.

"I don't know," he admitted. "Security, I guess. Can't breathe, can't swim—you gotta hold onto something."

Terry lifted the bloody, sopping Kleenex. "You *can* bounce, though," she said. "Hits like these should've broken your skull open."

"I'm the guy who started the day getting punched in the head and kicked out of a bomber," he said. "A few stalactites are child's play."

After giving his leg a reassuring pat, Terry walked to the river, took off her shoes, removed her remaining sock, and soaked it with fresh river water. She took a moment to enjoy the sun glistening on the river, the feathery branches of the many tamarisk plants, and the butterflies fluttering just above the newly bloomed wildflowers near the shore. Then she came back and dabbed at the wound.

Hale put his hand under his head. "Are *you* all right?" he asked.

She nodded.

"You don't look it," he said.

"Okay, I'm not," she said. She started to cry in big, heaving sobs.

With effort, Hale sat and put his arms around her. "If it's any consolation, I'm not either."

"It's no consolation," she said. "This sucks."

"I know, Terry, but we're going to get through it."

"But we just . . ." she said. "I mean, we almost . . ."

"I know."

"A nuclear bomb went off," she said.

"That it did," Hale said comfortingly.

"So are we—I mean—"

He smiled pleasantly. "Uh-uh," he said, and pointed to the butterflies. "Look, if the butterflies are healthy, then we are, too."

She cocked her head and sniffed back her tears. "Really?"

"Absolutely." He was still smiling. "It says so in the manual. 'If you see butterflies after a detonation, you're fine.'"

She frowned. "You're an asshole."

"That's Mr. Asshole to you."

"Seriously," Terry said, "we haven't been—uh, sterilized or anything like that?"

He smiled and pulled a small yellow disc from inside his collar and held it up to her face. "See this?"

She made an "of course" face.

"They sew these into our uniforms," Hale said. "If there were radiation, it would turn blue. So would we, for that matter." He wiggled it back and forth. "But it's not blue. It's yellow. And we're not coughing up blood and doubled over with pain."

She relaxed a little.

"The only things that'll get hurt by the blast are radios and computers," Hale said. "The electromagnetism'll knock the shit out of them. Our gene pool will come through unscathed."

"That's a relief," Terry said. She sat back and threw the sock at him. "Now take care of your own wound, Mr. Asshole."

He did, and then they stared at each other for a moment and started laughing.

"We're hungry, cold, and there's a nutcase out there with a nuclear bomb," Terry said. "What the hell are we doing?"

"Enjoying being alive," Hale said. "That's no small thing."

"I guess not," Terry said. She looked around at the splendor of the park. It had swallowed the blast and was still here, its countless parts still alive. Hale was right: that *was* no small thing.

With Terry's help, Hale rose slowly. He leaned against a boulder, and while he found his legs, Terry took off her blouse and wrung it out.

"Don't look," she said.

"Why not?" Hale asked. "I'm too damn weak to do anything."

Terry turned her back to him, but felt his eyes on her just the same. She didn't mind: in fact, she had to admit she liked it.

She knew she was in very good shape, and since her last boy-friend of five years walked out on her—no one had bothered to watch her change. Even when she walked into the bedroom shower naked, her boyfriend hadn't looked up from his cross-word puzzle.

"Y'know," Hale said, "there's something I've been meaning to ask you."

"Ask," she said.

Hale began checking his wet automatic. "How did someone like you end up with a gun?"

Terry turned her head back and glared at him. "What do you mean, 'someone like me'?"

"Nothing bad—I mean, of your sensibilities. I saw the way you looked at the butterflies, and at the river. I listened to you hum Chopin as we walked."

Her face registered surprise. "You like him?"

"I grew to. My mom was the fanatic. She played his nocturnes and waltzes all night, every night, while my dad was arguing politics with friends. I would never have pictured her with a gun. So how'd it happen with you?"

Terry put the seriously wrinkled shirt back on and turned around. "It happened after I hit a bank robber with a frozen chicken."

"Excuse me?" Hale said.

She planted her backside on the rock beside Hale. "I started out as a cook on rafting trips through here in the summer. Eventually, I became a guide. When a park ranger job opened up, I applied. See, I thought that being a ranger was going to mean leading nature hikes and finding lost kids. Instead, it's breaking up fights and rescuing idiots who climb something and then can't get down."

"I'm still waiting for the chicken."

"Right." She smiled. "The local Parks Department people didn't want to hire me. They weren't sure how I'd do with the law enforcement part of the job. Well, one night I was coming home from the store and Danny Lee—part of the local brain trust—was robbing old Anita Mui in front of the ATM. I heard Anita yelling and I saw Danny heading for his car, so I tossed a bag of groceries at him while going thirty miles an hour. A frozen chicken in the bag hit Danny in his least vulnerable spot, the forehead, but he dropped anyway. Next thing I know, I'm a ranger."

Hale looked at Terry with what was clearly fresh appreciation. "Real 'Who was that masked man?' type stuff."

"Yeah," she said. "The Lone Park Ranger, that's me."

She looked down, felt Hale's eyes on her again, liked it just as much as before, and thought how nice it felt when he'd held her.

Hale poked her arm with his thumb. "We better get moving. We'll warm up faster."

He stood and seemed surprised when he didn't fall.

"You gonna be all right?" Terry asked.

Hale nodded. "Now for the final *Jeopardy* answer: Deakins. The question: what chance do we have of catching up with him?"

"Pretty good, actually," Terry said. "We're on the Riverbank Trail, which goes along the river but twenty to thirty feet above it. It happens to be good for feet but bad for Humvees. To get out of the park, Deakins is going to have to stick to the main trail—something that's going to cost him a lot of time. Even though he's had a jump on us, we can head him off at the pass."

"Sounds good," Hale said. "Lead on."

Terry pushed off the rock. She waited for Hale to do likewise.

"Just so you know," Terry said, "I've never been along this trail."

"Just so you know," Hale shot back, "with your track record so far, that's a relief."

Terry scowled, though the twinkle in his eye belied the malice of his words.

With the morning sun baking their wet shirts and warming them quickly, they started out at a brisk pace, Terry hoping for the captain's sake that they found the man who had betrayed him . . . while selfishly hoping for her sake that they didn't.

47

The walk to the rock took twenty-five minutes.

The drive to the lanky man with the Uzi took seven minutes longer.

The rock was a boulder on the Riverbank Trail, one which was large enough to conceal both Terry and Hale. They hid behind it after spotting the long, heavy-duty zodiac raft tied to a tree on the riverbank. The man with the Israeli-made submachine gun was sitting on its stiff rubber side, smoking a cigarette. There was an empty pallet behind him, tarps bunched up on the far side, and a long crate marked *Life Jackets* strapped to one of the side pontoons.

"Think he's gunning for fish?" Terry asked.

Hale didn't answer. He was looking down the river at an approaching cloud of dust. Whatever was causing it was hidden by the ledge they were on.

"Get me a frozen Zacky's fryer," Terry said, "and he's a dead man."

Now they both heard the engine of the vehicle that was causing the dust cloud. It stopped out of sight — where the wide trail ended, Terry guessed, about four hundred yards from the river.

"We used to talk about continuing it," Terry said, "but were afraid that'd scare the fish and fowl. It's bad enough people can get here and cut their initials in the cacti."

Hale knew that Terry was talking because she was nervous, but that was fine. Deakins wouldn't be able to hear them up here.

The man in the raft flicked his cigarette into the river and rose. He walked briskly toward Deakins, who had come into view and was approaching more slowly. Hale could tell his ex-partner was tired, and that made him feel good: despite being ejected, nearly exploded, and coming a few breaths shy of drowned, he was surprisingly energized.

"Good morning, Mr. Sheppard," Deakins said with mock courtliness.

"Mornin'." The tall, lean man looked past Deakins at the Humvee. "Where is everyone?"

"I *am* everyone."

"Something happen?" the man drawled.

"Yes," Deakins said. He fixed his eyes on Sheppard. "They asked too many dumb questions."

"Oh," Sheppard said. "Gotcha."

The two men turned and walked back toward the Humvee.

Terry said to Hale, "Bet you I know what they're going to get."

Hale nodded. He was looking at the raft, the Humvee, and the path that led from their crude but effective hiding place to the river.

Terry asked, "So when does the cavalry get here?"

"We have to assume they don't."

Terry's brow knit. "What do you mean? The Army would just let these nukes go, write them off like a bad debt?"

"No," Hale said. "But they may conclude that both bombs went off and the danger's over."

"That's a pretty big conclusion to jump to," Terry said. "I'd think you'd want to make *sure* with weapons like these."

"And they will," Hale said, "but only after a few dozen committee meetings at the Pentagon. The military only moves fast when they're at war."

Terry asked, "Aren't they?"

"They won't think so until they get Deakins's ultimatum," Hale said. "Which means right now, you and I are the only good guys who know for sure what's going on."

"Yea for us," she said. "So what do we do? Looks like there's just two of them. Even odds."

Hale waited until Deakins and Sheppard were out of sight, then said, "We can't risk attacking them and losing. We want to be smart about this."

"Why start now?" Terry said.

"I'm serious." Hale scowled.

"You think I'm not?"

"The first thing we want to do is strand them," Hale said. "We get the raft and take ourselves a little Proud Mary roll down the river."

"Why not just sink it, or disable it?"

"Because they may be able to salvage it," Hale said. "You ready?"

Terry nodded.

Moving out from behind the boulder, Hale led her down the path toward the shore. They paused where the trail and path met, then looked ahead and made sure Deakins and Sheppard were where they thought they were.

They were. They were offloading the nuke and planning to carry it to the raft.

"Okay," Hale whispered. "Let's do it."

The two rushed to the raft, unseen by Deakins and Sheppard, who were busy with the bomb. They climbed in and Hale put his hand on the engine throttle in back.

"Shit!" he said.

"What?" she asked.

"Keys!" he said, as though it were an oath.

The two of them looked around the raft, then Terry pointed to a duffel bag lying on the riverbank.

"Maybe there," she said.

Hale leaped out, grimacing as he landed on a cut or bruise he had not known about until just then. He turned the bag over, shook the contents out, then tore through them. He threw aside Snickers bars, a Walkman, and a hunting knife. He dug through clothes and crap and didn't find a key.

He was just about to fish through the empty bag when he heard grunting and small, fast steps along the rocky riverbank.

Damn, Hale thought.

He looked for a place to hide, saw none, and rolled into the river, which was the fastest, least noisy way he could think of to get in. Just before he went under, he saw Terry get up—but though he watched for a telltale splash, he never saw her enter the water. Maybe she slipped in delicately. He hoped so; if she tried to get back to the path, she'd never make it.

Hale let the current carry him ahead, and then grabbed the sheer line on the far side of the raft.

Hale hung there, his nose just above the water, listening. He heard nothing except the heavy-breathing men as they reached the raft and hoisted the bomb in. The zodiac bobbed deeply and stayed down.

"That was fun," Sheppard panted. "Now, tell me—why were you driving around with a dead guy?"

Deakins was also breathing heavily. "Because," he replied, "I like him. *He* doesn't ask a lot of questions."

"Right," Sheppard said. "I forgot. Well, at least a body doesn't need a road map to find where you're at."

"Let's hope you don't need a road map to find Max,"

Deakins said menacingly. "I want to reach him before my friends in Washington get their candygram."

Hale heard the distinctive rustling of one of the tarps—they were covering the bomb, no doubt—and a few seconds later the engine purred contentedly. Hale ducked under the water as the raft took off over him. He surfaced just in time to watch it scoot into the distance.

Terry was nowhere to be seen.

48

Baird had two pet peeves. One was smelling of b.o. and the other was having food stuck between his teeth.

He usually slipped a stick of deodorant and a pack of waxed dental floss inside his suit pocket so he could use them when his own odorous, omnivorous, animal nature started to bother him.

He didn't need to floss right now; he'd only had coffee since he got here. But after the videotape arrived in a box that said *Candygram for Mr. Mongo*, whoever that was, he wished he could have slipped away and coated his underarms. He was sweating like a hippo.

For the second time, everyone in the crowded room—anti-terrorist experts from the military, the FBI, and the CIA had been brought in—was forced to watch a camcorder view of downtown Salt Lake City, with Deakins standing dead center.

Deakins, Baird thought. These bozos had been wrong about that, too. He and Hale were in this together.

Baird phased back in as Deakins was saying, ". . . two hundred and fifty million dollars by nine A.M., Utah time. The depositing instructions are in the envelope that came with this tape. If you're smart and you get the money from the Pentagon's secret programs, no one ever has to know about this."

"He's so damned considerate," muttered Schneider.

"One thing to keep in mind, though," Deakins continued. "This deadline is not negotiable, and there is no grace period. The device is on a timer. Shortly after you receive this, the timer will be activated. At nine-zero-one, I will make a call. If I find out that you've done as you've been instructed, I will stop the timer. If you have not complied, or if at any point you attempt to stop me from getting the device to Salt Lake City—well, I've already set off one bomb. I can set off another. And then—"

Now the corny showman kicks in, Baird thought. Deakins had edited together a flurry of images of nuclear destruction— buildings, ships, trees, and tanks being obliterated, mushroom clouds erupting, fires burning, Godzilla stomping through a city. Baird looked away. He didn't need to see it again.

Obviously, Dryfoos didn't either. "Turn that thing off," the chairman ordered.

An assistant complied. Men shifted in seats. Breath was exhaled. And finally, Baird spoke.

"I guess the first question to ask is, can we get the money in time?"

Dryfoos said, "Yes."

General Creeley leaned forward. "But we won't. I think I speak for most of the people in this room when I say that we can't capitulate to terrorists, whether they're foreign or home-grown."

"And who speaks for the people of Salt Lake City?" Dryfoos asked.

"We do," Creeley said. "And what they'd say, if anyone bothered to ask them, is 'No. We won't be threatened.'"

"Ask them again when the question isn't so abstract," Baird

said, "and the timer's at ten, nine, eight seconds to zero. I think you'd get a different answer."

"I don't," Creeley said. "I've faced bullets and artillery. Have you? Did they shoot at you at N.Y.U., Mr. International Relations Ph.D.?"

"Here, here." Schneider thumped the table with his knuckles.

"Let's stow the personal stuff," Dryfoos said.

"Sorry, sir," Creeley said, though Baird could tell he wasn't. "All I'm saying is, my resolve didn't change just because my ass was on the firing line."

"That's just my point!" Baird said. "If the bomb were in this room, I'd have no problem telling Deakins, 'Up yours.' But it isn't my ass or your ass. It's a whole lot of innocent people who expect their government to protect them, not to let them be used as pawns."

Creeley made a disgusted face and swept an arm across the table. "You've got a room full of antiterrorist experts. Ask them what they'd do. Ask them what they think of the precedent we'd be setting."

"What precedent?" Baird asked. "Deakins thought of that, didn't he? No one ever has to know about this."

"That's bullshit," Creeley said. "He'll crow about it to anyone who'll listen. He'll get a friggin' book deal, write it from his villa in Spain. Maybe he'll even give goddamn lessons in nuclear terrorism for a percentage of the take."

"I think you're getting a little carried away," Baird said. "He just wants to get rich and go away."

"No," Creeley said. "Every pilot's got some thrill seeker in him. This man—this maniac—won't just go away." Creeley turned to Dryfoos. "Sir, Deakins is one of my own, a flyboy. Let me deal with him. In ten minutes I can put up a wall of men and machines fifty miles from Salt Lake that a fly couldn't get through."

"But he said the bomb would go off if we tried to stop him," Baird reminded him.

"Yes, *he* said that," Creeley agreed. "What do you expect him to say? He can't have gotten it in there already—the damn thing hasn't been in his hands long enough!"

"And how do we know he even still has a bomb?" Schneider noted. "He made that tape long before McMurran felt the underground blast. For all we know, the guy's got nothing but hot air."

"Eighteen million degrees Fahrenheit hot," said Baird.

Dryfoos said, "I agree with Mr. Baird. What if he *has* got a bomb and a way to deliver it? And what if he uses it?"

"People will sympathize," Creeley said. "They'll understand that we had the backbone to stand up to a madman."

Dryfoos said, "I'm not worried about how we're perceived. I'm worried about people dying—a lot of them fast, a lot of them more slowly, all of them horribly."

Baird looked at his watch. "Fortunately or unfortunately, this isn't our decision. We've got to inform the President."

"Along with our recommendation," Dryfoos said.

"Correct," said Baird. "I'm going to suggest that we work with Deakins. Mr. Chairman?"

Dryfoos thought for a moment. "It's not that I think you're wrong." He nodded toward Creeley and Schneider. "And I can tell from the faces of many of our other guests that they agree with you."

The representatives from the other agencies did not disagree.

"However," Dryfoos said, "in this case I'm going to recommend that we put lives before pride. We should pay the son of a bitch."

Creeley pursed his lips and folded his hands tightly. "What about the President's standing?" he asked, playing it hard, like an ace on a jack in a game of twenty-one.

Baird was stunned. "What about it?"

"He's at forty-seven percent in the polls," Creeley said. "Telling terrorists to go screw themselves is good for ten to fifteen points."

"And what'll losing a city cost him?" Baird asked with disgust.

"Truthfully? Nothing. People rally around the chief executive in times of trouble. Good for ten points. Jimmy Carter was in the toilet until the hostages were taken in Iran. Result? He beats back a presidential challenge from Ted Kennedy. Clinton was in the bowl until Oklahoma City was attacked. Result? Big gain in the polls. Crises force presidents to lead, and people respond to leadership."

"You're incredible," Baird said. "You can't get in the front door, so you try the back."

"Hell, I'll try the rotating doggy door if I have to. You guys are making a mistake and, frankly, I'm not as sure as you are that the President will buy what you're selling."

Baird took a deep breath and reached for the phone. "Very well, then. Let's find out, shall we?"

49

Hale should have felt good, or at least he should have felt a *hint* of good. But he didn't. He'd failed the only person who'd been there for him, and it was weighing heavily on him.

Hurrying back to shore after the raft left, he'd begun running along the riverbank, hoping to find someone with a car or a boat or even a bicycle. There was no one, though as his churning legs began to cramp and his chest began to ache, he came upon a marina that rented houseboats—and, outside of it, a blue sign with the white silhouette of a telephone.

Forty minutes later, six army helicopters were landing near the marina. Two men hopped from the first one to touch down, and ran over to Hale.

"Captain Hale," Wilkins said as he approached the shack.

"Colonel." Hale saluted.

"Captain, this is Giles Prentice," Wilkins said, "assistant chief of staff to the President."

Hale's eyes shifted to Giles. Wilkins he knew and liked; this kid he didn't know and wasn't sure he liked, just by looking at him.

Hale's eyes said as much, and Giles picked up on it. The

newcomer was smart enough to offer his hand and remain silent.

"We were surprised to get your call," Wilkins went on, seemingly oblivious to what had passed between the two. "Some people had you pegged as the perpetrator."

Hale was still looking at Giles. "Anyone we know?"

Giles looked away.

"Anyway," Hale said quickly, "nice of them to think I had the smarts."

"Smarts?" Wilkins said with disgust. "You think Deakins is smart?"

"In a sick sort of way, sir. Yes, sir."

"This is deviousness, utterly evil and demented," Wilkins said.

"What about the raft?" Hale asked, eager to change the subject.

"We found it on the other side of the lake," the colonel said. "Tracks from a heavy truck ran out when they hit the paved road."

"Any sign of the ranger?" Hale asked.

Wilkins shook his head. "No. Sorry."

Hale's eyes dropped. "We're wasting time, then. I assume you've got a rad scanner so we can track them?"

Wilkins and Giles swapped looks.

"Actually, Captain," Wilkins said, "we're not part of the search-and-destroy team. The three of us are going back to McMurran."

Hale's eyes snapped back up. "What?"

Giles said, "We'd just like to ask you a few questions."

"Hey, who the hell *are* you, anyway?"

"The colonel told you—"

"No," Hale said, stepping closer. "I mean, who the hell are *you* to ask me questions? I had nothing to do with this, except to have my ass in the way of Deakins's boot in the air, on the ground, and in the water. I'm not going to waste time answering questions when we've got an utterly evil and demented jerkoff running around with an A-bomb."

Giles smirked and took a step closer himself. "Captain Hale. You can come with us, or"—he threw a thumb over his shoulder—"you can go with them."

Hale looked at the chopper that had landed nearest to them. Four immaculate MPs had gotten out. From their shades to their sidearms to their spread-legged posture, they were decked out to rumble.

The captain glared at Giles. His own tailor-made uniform, crisp and bright just hours before, was now stiff and wrinkled from muck, water, dirt, and sweat. Yet he felt cleaner than this self-important Nathan Thurm of a bureaucrat.

Hale looked at Wilkins. "Colonel, I'm the guy who called you. Why would I do that if—"

"I don't know," Wilkins cut him off impatiently. "As I said, some people had you pegged as a perpetrator . . . and some people still do. I'm sorry, Captain, but you're under arrest."

"Arrest?"

"That's right," Giles said.

Hale ignored him. It was either that or kill him. He continued to look at Wilkins. "Colonel, let's find the ranger and *then* I'll go. Please. If she were one of your men, you'd do anything to get her back."

Wilkins looked at his watch. "Hale, the President has opted to stand up to Major Deakins. We're going to have twenty thousand troops on the ground within fifteen minutes. We *are* going to stop them."

"But if you stop him, she's as good as dead."

"We've got sharpshooters."

"*If* you can get to him," Hale said.

Wilkins motioned for Hale to head for the helicopter. He did, with the petulance of a kid being sent to his room. The colonel fell in between Hale and Giles.

"Sir," said Hale, "I don't think anyone really understands what's happening here."

"You do, though—"

"Only because I flew beside the bastard for years, Colonel. I know how his mind works. Deakins has this planned out. He'll blow that thing if you come at him hard. The ranger will die, along with a few thousand other people."

"We don't know that," Wilkins said.

"Yes you do. And worse, you don't care."

Wilkins glared at him. "Captain—"

"All right, maybe *you* do," Hale corrected himself, "and maybe that's why you're not happy to be here. You aren't, are you?"

Wilkins stopped glaring and looked away. Hale stepped ahead of the other two and walked backward in front of the colonel.

"Tell me I'm wrong, sir," he said. "We take Deakins out in middle-of-nowhere Wayne County, where the population's not so dense, and if the nuke goes, it goes. We lose deer and wildcats and the people of Hanksville and Fruita and whoever else is living where the wind blows. Tough stance on terrorism. Regrettable losses and all that, but unavoidable."

"The United States government does not consider the loss of civilian lives acceptable," Wilkins said.

"I didn't say acceptable," Hale told him, "I said regrettable. And don't feed me the party line, sir. I know how this drill works—we both do. In a hostage situation, a rescue is considered successful even with a ten percent loss of life. There're nearly a million people in Salt Lake City—you do the math."

"Please get in, Captain," Giles said as they reached the chopper.

Hale glared at him. "You're a suit, so maybe all this is okay with you." He looked at Wilkins. "But we're military officers, Colonel. We took an oath. Those weapons and the safety of that civilian are our responsibility. Now, you want to send me to

Leavenworth for a thousand years starting tomorrow A.M., that's fine with me. But right now, sir, as one officer to another, we have a duty to bring this episode to a close."

Wilkins and Hale stared at each other. Hale felt like he had the colonel somewhere close to where he wanted him.

"Sir," Hale said, "all I'm asking is the chance to finish what I started here. Give me two hours. Come with me. You've served in the field—"

"I can't," Wilkins said. "The deadline's nine A.M., which is less than two hours from now."

"Fine, give me one hour. I can *do* this!"

Giles said, "The crisis management team is not prepared to turn this matter over to an Air Force major who may or may not have a hard-on for his partner."

Hale said, "I'm gonna punch you, pissant."

"You will not," Wilkins said. He took a deep breath. "Captain Hale, I have orders to return you to McMurran. You understand what orders are, don't you, Captain?"

"Yes, sir," Hale said gloomily.

"Good," Wilkins said. "Because we're going to break them."

Hale looked at him. "Sir?"

"Are you hard of hearing?" Wilkins asked.

"Actually, yes, sir." Hale smiled. "But thank you, sir."

Wilkins looked at Giles. "Any argument, Mr. Prentice?"

"Would it do any good if I had one?" Giles asked. Now he was the one who was gloomy.

"Frankly, it wouldn't," Wilkins said.

Giles shrugged. "Then no, Colonel. I have no argument."

The men started jogging toward the helicopter and Giles looked at Hale.

"And for the record, Captain, I'm not 'just' a suit. I was a reserve lieutenant in the ROTC. Two years. Yale."

"New Haven *is* a war zone," Wilkins said.

Hale gave Giles a half smile. "So now we're the Three Musketeers," he said. "Let's kick ass then, shall we?"

205

50

Dusty slices of light passed through the slatted walls of the open rear of the trunk. It turned the steel D-rings into gleaming circles of silver, and what was lashed between them, a weblike black hammock, into a shadow that cast more shadows on the floor of the truck.

Except where the bomb was. It cast a solid shadow, like a stubby pencil, amid the network of dark lines.

Deakins stood over the nuclear bomb that lay on the hammock. Though the bomb caused the fibers to stretch and strain, they kept it relatively steady as the truck sped down the empty stretch of highway. That had enabled them to stay on the move as Max attached the timer.

Sitting cross-legged in front of him, his blue eyes peering out from his leathery, weatherbeaten face, Max was keying numbers into the electronic timer. The short, trim man's eyes were partially obscured by his longish, dirty blond hair. Deakins wondered how the hell he could see.

Deakins heard the distinctive cry of a bird of prey, and Max jumped as there was a sudden flutter of wings and wild clucking.

"You know, Colonel," Max said, "I usually do work like this in a dirt-free, not to mention chicken-free, environment."

"For what I'm paying you, you should be able to do it one-handed in a dust storm." Deakins looked around. "Besides, I think it adds to the ambience."

Max sneered into his flannel sleeve. "How's that?"

Deakins looked up at the canvas covering on the truck and thought of the canvas floor in a boxing ring. It was a fitting full circle—one a symbol of his poor Hell's Kitchen youth, the other a symbol of the riches that were about to pour down on him.

"What?" Deakins said. "Oh, you wanted to know about the ambience? Well, feathers are flying. Frightened birds are squawk-ing. It prepares us spiritually for what is about to transpire."

"You have the soul of a poet," Max observed.

"That I do." Deakins smiled.

Max said, "You want it set for nine-oh-five, correct?"

Deakins nodded.

Max checked his watch. "That's exactly twenty-three minutes from now. You're sure you don't want more of a window?"

Deakins said, "Don't need it. Besides, I promised the folks in Washington . . . and I wouldn't want to let them down."

Max set the timer and stood, straightening slowly. "I remember when I used to be able to hop right up."

"You can buy yourself some therapy," Deakins said. He went the front of the cargo area. He stopped where the canvas covering reached the cab. "I'm going to join Sheppard and the boys. You stay here."

"And do what?" Max asked.

Deakins said, "Watch."

"What?"

The major grinned. "The chickens. Who knows? We might get breakfast."

51

The Black Hawk moved north as Lieutenant Lynne Dominick looked for signs of anything that wasn't a bird, tree, quadruped, or rock. So far, those were all she'd seen.

Then the detector to the right of the pilot bleeped and then it bleeped faster. The arrow on the circular green map on top pointed to the northwest.

"There," said the black-haired officer as she saw the truck that said Rodriguez and Sons on the side.

The chopper banked sharply and descended as it bore down on the truck.

"That's got to be it," said Dominick. "There's nothing else around."

The Black Hawk leveled off and flew low over the treetops toward the otherwise deserted highway. As it neared, the bleeps went from one every two seconds to three each second.

"Knock on the door," the lieutenant said to the copilot.

The copilot-gunner leaned forward and looked into the multipurpose sighting system in the center of the instrument panel. On either side were handgrips which operated the twin M-60 side-firing machine guns.

The Black Hawk strafed the truck, punching holes in the

canvas top and clanging off the metal support ribs. When the bullets struck the side of the cab, the passenger's side window shattered and the truck swerved. Regaining control of the vehicle, the driver hit the accelerator.

"You can't outrun a helicopter," Lieutenant Dominick said under her breath. "Get in front of him and turn around," she ordered the pilot.

The tail of the Black Hawk rose and the chopper forged ahead, passing the truck. When it was nearly a quarter mile ahead, it turned and hovered ten feet above the asphalt, facing the truck.

"Stop him," she said to the copilot.

As the truck approached, the guns chewed into the front tires and grille. The driver's side tire exploded, flinging rubber shards behind it, and the truck veered to that side. It sped from the highway into a ditch and up the other side, and spun to a stop in the dirt.

The chopper inched over as the driver got out with his hands up.

"I give!" he shouted as the copilot and Lieutenant Dominick emerged, automatics tucked under their arms. "Oh, I do give. Uncle. I fold."

"Higher," said Dominick, motioning with the gun barrel, "and move away from the truck."

"You're callin' the shots—me in the corner pocket, whatever you say." The grizzled driver walked away as he stretched his arms to their fullest height. "What is this, some kinda invasion? You guys foreigners or paramilitaries? Not that I care. I'm your prisoner. Name, rank, serial number, and anything else I know—it's yours."

"Just stay where you are," the lieutenant said as the copilot walked to the back of the truck.

He reached out and got ready to pull aside the flap. When Dominick nodded, the copilot drew it aside and pointed his weapon at the driver; as he did so, Dominick shifted her gun from the driver to the back of the truck, which she was better positioned to cover.

The back of the truck was empty save for a small canister. Lieutenant Dominick peered with astonishment through her sunglasses.

"What does it say?" she asked the copilot.

He leaned into the back of the truck. "It says, *Radioactive waste, St. Jude's Department of Radiology.*"

"Radiation?" the driver said. "Shee-it! Am I gonna goddamn glow in the dark?"

Lieutenant Dominick walked toward him. She stopped just a few paces away, could smell the combination of liquor and coffee on his breath. "Are you trying to tell me you didn't know what was in there?"

"I *am* tellin' ya that, yes ma'am—I mean, Officer. Ma'am. Sir."

"How could you not know?"

"Truck says produce, I figger it's produce. Ole Sammy Lawrence, he don't ask questions."

"How did you come by it?" She glanced at the side. "From Mr. Rodriguez?"

"I don't know who he was. I work at Woog's Diner outside St. George, I finished my shift on the grill, and some guy offers me a hunnert bucks to drive his truck to Salt Lake. Hey, a hunnert bucks is a hunnert bucks. Cash. But—shit, hell, o'course, I'll report it on my taxes. Anyhow, that's how it happened. I swear!

"What guy was this?" she said.

"I dunno. One of your kinda guys. I mean, he had a flight suit an' all. Kinda dirty, like he'd been flippin' burgers or grease monkeyin'."

Lieutenant Dominick instructed the man to sit down with his hands on his head, told the copilot to stay with him, then went back to the chopper. The radios were still out, so she would have to go back to the houseboat rental office and use the telephone.

Someone had pulled a sleight of hand, and she had a feeling it was going to cost them all dearly.

52

Hale was sitting in the back of the helicopter with Colonel Wilkins to his right. Giles was in front of the colonel, next to the pilot, Captain Chan. A map was spread across the laps of Hale and Wilkins.

Since they'd taken off five minutes before, Hale had been looking at the map, looking out the window, looking back at the map, then looking back out the window.

"I don't know what you're looking for, Captain," Wilkins said. "We've sealed every road between here and Salt Lake."

Hale's mind was moving like the chopper rotor, fast and always coming back to the same place.

"Major Deakins would have expected you to do that," Hale said.

"So?" said Wilkins. "That means he's either got to lay low, punch through, or fly out. In any case, we'll get him."

"I'm not so certain about that," Hale said.

"What do you mean?"

"I mean, he's not going to sit still, and I don't think we'll find him on any roads."

"Sorry, Captain," Wilkins said. "You lost me."

Hale tapped the map. "Is this what you issued to guys setting up the roadblocks?"

Wilkins nodded. "Standard military issue."

"With a revision date six months old," Hale said.

"Right," said Wilkins. "It's new."

"So new," said Hale, "that you didn't bother to put things on that were old and obsolete."

"Such as?" asked Giles.

Hale pointed outside his window. Wilkins and Giles both leaned over.

"Train tracks," said Wilkins.

"It's obviously an old spur," said Hale. "Covered with weeds and beer bottles. Probably hasn't been used in twenty years, so nobody bothered to put it on the new map."

"Boots and saddles!" said Wilkins.

"Amen," said Hale. "The nuke isn't in a truck, Colonel. It's on a train."

Wilkins looked at him with disbelief that quickly shaded from understanding to alarm. "Hell, that's why he was so goddamn confident."

The colonel told the pilot to try the radio again. He picked up the microphone, clicked it on, spoke, clicked off to wait, then repeated. After five attempts, he shook his head.

"It's still down, sir."

Wilkins rolled his lips together. "We'll have to check this out. Pilot, head north along the tracks. We'll see if there's a—"

"No," Hale said suddenly. "Go south."

"But Salt Lake is north," Giles said.

"I know," said Hale. "But I'm starting to think our friend isn't going to Salt Lake. I know this guy. If everything points to him heading north, then he's probably heading south."

"Probably?" Wilkins said. "You want us to pin our response on a 'probably'?"

"No," Hale said after thinking about it, "Make it definitely. Deakins is definitely heading south."

"But *you* said it would be Salt Lake, too," Giles said. "On the phone, you said you found that hospital tag."

Hale said, "Deakins planted that tag. He wanted whoever found it to think that's where he was going." The captain shook his head, angry that it had taken him this long to catch on. "The son of a bitch has been doing rope-a-dope."

Giles and Wilkins looked at each other and then back at Hale.

"Rope-a-dope?" said Giles.

"It's a boxing term," Hale said. "Ali in Zaire—it means a fakeout. Deakins admires the hell out of it."

"South," the Colonel said. "What could be south of here that would interest Deakins?"

Hale watched as Wilkins's index finger followed a course to the south, across the border of Utah into Arizona.

"The Grand Canyon?" Wilkes said. "It's already a big hole. Nothing to gain by hitting that, Captain."

Hale studied the map. Phoenix was about three hundred miles to the south. Albuquerque was the same distance to the southeast. And Las Vegas was three hundred miles to the southwest.

"Las Vegas," Hale said with disgust. "What the hell is there to blow up in Las Vegas?"

Giles straightened up in his seat. "Oh my God," he said.

Hale and Wilkins both looked at him.

"What's wrong?" asked Hale.

"What you just said—"

"You mean, what the hell is there to blow up in Las Vegas?"

Giles nodded. He ran his tongue over his lips, then said, "Gentlemen: the President is in Las Vegas."

53

The freight train was thundering through the flatlands, a diesel engine pulling three boxcars with doors on all four sides. It was followed by a flatcar loaded with oil drums, a boxcar with a satellite dish, a flatcar with a Red Cross helicopter lashed securely by cables, and a caboose.

Until today, the scariest sensory input Terry had ever experienced was a 3-D Imax movie she'd seen during a park rangers convention in New York. The second scariest was when she was cabbed to Madison Square Garden the next morning, when hockey playoff tickets went on sale. The hack who drove her thought she had wanted to see *those* Rangers.

But today Terry had hitched a dirty, bumpy ride on the back of a truck, had hidden inside a suffocating crate filled with life jackets for a sickening raft ride, and now was holding on to the side ladder of a train racing through the hinterlands of God-knew-where.

She assumed that the military would figure out where they were. That being the case, this seemed like the perfect time to slip into the engine and try to overcome whoever was inside. All Terry had going for her was a green belt in jujitsu and the hopefully-not-overrated element of surprise. As she moved from the ladder to the side-door sliding channel to the ladder on the other side, she prayed that was enough.

Terry opened the door between the grab irons, twisted the handle, and pulled slowly. She saw two men inside. One of them was wearing a trainman's cap. He was looking out the front window, doing nothing. The other was holding a Colt Commando submachine gun.

Terry entered cautiously and looked around for something to use as a weapon. She saw a heavy flashlight on the wall. As she reached for it, it came away from the tension hook with a loud *k-ching*.

Max turned. "Hey! Who the hell are you?"

Instead of answering, Terry swung the flashlight at him. He ducked and she hit the trainman on the bridge of his nose. He fell, dazed.

Max used the butt of the gun to knock the flashlight away. As Terry stepped back and assumed her fighting position—right arm cocked back hard, in chamber, left fist raised shoulder-high—Max stepped in fast with his gun butt. He faked toward her chest then jabbed toward her knee and she hit it back with a knee-kick. But standing on one leg in the rattling train caused her to lose her balance. As she stumbled to the right, Max nailed her on the left side of the head with the gun butt. She dropped straight to the engine floor.

"Thought I was just Choo-Choo Charlie, huh?" Max leered as he moved in on her. He held his thumb up. "Well, Cynthia Rothrock, it so happens that I was a Navy SEAL. Three tours of duty. You should see what I can do with just one itty bitty finger."

Terry's left ear was singing. But she was alert enough to realize that she had landed on the flashlight. Her right hand was underneath her. Wrapping her fingers around the light, she whipped it out and flung it in the same swift motion. The battery-heavy rear end caught Max square in the forehead and he dropped next to the trainman.

Terry got back on her feet. "Yeah?" she said triumphantly. "Well, Mr. SEAL, you should see what *I* can do with just a chicken."

As Terry walked toward the far side of the compartment, Max made a sudden grab for her left ankle. With a shout, she brought her right heel down hard on his wrist and he withdrew it with a yelp. She snatched up the Colt, rose, and pointed it down at him.

"Are we finished playing yet?" Terry asked.

Max touched his bloody forehead. He nodded. Terry stole a glance at the trainman. He appeared to be down for the count.

"You know how to operate this train?" she asked.

Max nodded.

"Good. I want you to stop it."

"Fuck you," he said.

Terry drew back the Colt's hammer. "I've had a rough day. Now, either you're going to stop the goddamn train, or you'll be playing a harp, SEAL."

Max got on his knees. "Okay, okay, you win," he said. He touched his forehead gingerly. "Just lemme take care of this."

Before Terry could say anything, Max reached into his pocket and withdrew a handkerchief. Suddenly, the white cloth fell away and Max lunged at her with a switchblade.

She didn't try to knock it away. There wasn't time. Instead, she fired at his chest.

Max didn't fly back, like in the movies. He fell forward, twisting onto his side, the knife falling from his hand. If he made a sound, she didn't hear it because of the noise of the train. His eyes moved from side to side for a moment, and he gasped for a few seconds. Then he went limp and his eyes shut.

Terry's lower lip trembled and she dropped to her knees. She set the gun down.

There wasn't a choice, she told herself. This man was going to kill her.

Still, she had killed some mother's child and that made her want to vomit.

She looked away, and as she did she saw the brake and accelerator levers. She walked over to the levers on her knees. *Focus,* she told herself. *You still have a job to do.*

As she tried to determine which was which, she realized that it didn't matter. She understood why the trainman had been standing there doing nothing. There were large globs of solid metal along their bases. Both levers had been welded into place.

The train could not be stopped.

54

A hatch opened on the roof of the boxcar next to the flatcar, and Deakins climbed halfway out. He looked at the small microwave dish next to the hatchway and grinned.

You do think of everything, he thought. He cast his eyes skyward. There were no choppers. No Air Force. No Hale.

No clue, he thought with satisfaction as he ducked back inside. Even if the Air Force had already found the truck, they would be too late to stop what he had set in motion.

It had all worked just as it was supposed to. Max had conked out a bunch of yokel engineers and stolen the train for him, and the engineer they'd hired showed up right on schedule. After the bomb had been transferred—along with the chicken crates, just in cast they were stopped by some yokel trooper or railroad cop for some dumbshit inspection—Max had driven the truck with its decoy to St. George, hired a driver, and joined them using the motorcycle he'd left at the diner earlier. Sheppard had welded the controls in the engine so the train couldn't be stopped.

The bottom line: all the hard work and planning and clandestine calls from Whiteman pay phones with pocketfuls of coins were about to pay off.

Deakins took a moment to enjoy the warm breeze, then ducked back inside. He climbed down the ladder that was attached to the front wall of the boxcar. The two shielded lightbulbs were swaying from side to side, making the shadows of the five men seem alive. In the other end of the boxcar were the chicken crates. Behind them, slung from its hammock, was the bomb.

Sheppard was lying on the floor of the boxcar, and his four men were playing poker nearby.

"These vibrations are relaxing as hell," Sheppard said to Deakins. "Y'oughta try it."

"Thanks, no," Deakins said.

"I bet it's like being back in the womb," Sheppard said. "Shaking and bobbing like this."

"That's a deep observation," Deakins said, "but let's save further philosophical discussions for the ride to Denmark."

"I'm not going to Denmark," Sheppard said. "I'm going to Orlando. Disneyworld."

"My loss," Deakins said ingenuously. He looked up at the sky and wondered why all flunkies, in fiction and in life, had the IQ of toast. Even those who were technically and militarily proficient, like Sheppard, were missing some key ingredients. As his nephew Wayne would've said, the state of affairs was both bogus and sad.

"When's dust-off?" Sheppard inquired.

Deakins looked at his watch. "Fifteen minutes. So I suggest you all—"

He stopped.

"We all what?" Sheppard asked,

"Shhh!" Deakins hissed. "Did you hear that?"

"Hear what?"

Deakins walked back to the ladder. He climbed and stuck his head through. After a moment, he hopped down the ladder backward.

"It sounded like a gunshot," Deakins said. He grabbed a walkie-talkie from one of the men and clicked on. "Max," he said, "is everything all right?"

Silence.

"Max," Deakins repeated, "call in."

Nothing.

Deakins swore. He snatched his automatic from where it was leaning against one of the chicken crates. "I'm going up front," he said. "If everything's okay, I'll blow the whistle once."

"What if it isn't okay?" Sheppard asked.

"Then I won't blow it at all," Deakins said. "Now listen. Even if someone has gotten onboard, we're still all right. We were going to radio Washington anyway. At this point, we pretty much expected the geniuses there to figure out where we are. But as long as we've got the bomb and can activate it, we're still in control. Got that?"

The men nodded, several of them halfheartedly. Deakins felt as if he were back in the ring with Hale, trying to teach him to fight. If he didn't need these guys, he'd have shot them where they stood.

"Trust me," said the major. "I haven't steered you wrong so far. Think about how you'll live it up when you're each worth three million." He looked at Sheppard. "Think of all the rides you can take at Epcot."

"Yeah, okay," said Sheppard.

Deakins headed toward the ladder. "You know the code," he said to Sheppard. "If you don't hear the whistle, arm the bomb and head for the chopper. I'll meet you there."

Sheppard nodded as Deakins climbed through the hatch and hurried toward the front of the speeding train.

55

Terry tried the levers, just to make sure they wouldn't move.

They wouldn't. But she was arm weary from clinging to the side of the train, and looked around for something to use as a lever—a crowbar or even a good strong screwdriver.

She stood and looked from the floor of the cabin to the walls of the window. And she gasped.

The edge of Deakins's face was showing through the open window. The edge of his face and the barrel of his gun.

"Put your hands on your head and turn around," Deakins said. "Slowly."

Terry obliged.

When she was facing away from him, Deakins opened the door and stepped in. He saw Max, kicked him with the toe of his boot. Then he smiled at Terry.

"You just saved me three million dollars," he said. "I owe you one."

Terry said, "Shoot yourself and we'll call it square."

Deakins turned her around and shook a finger at her. "You're an interesting person," he said. "Pesky, but interesting."

"Thanks. And you're twisted."

Deakins made a face. "Here I thought we had a mutual admiration thing going. Was I wrong?"

"You're off by about a light-year," Terry said. "It doesn't take talent to do what you're doing. Just balls."

"You're wrong about that," said Deakins. Still holding the gun on her, he walked over to the whistle and pulled the cord. "You may not approve of what I'm doing, but it took a lot of thought and ingenuity—"

"If you do say so yourself."

"Correct," said Deakins. He let go of the cord and walked back toward Terry. "Hell, I pulled this together without my partner and good friend finding out. Now *that* is a sub-rosa operation."

"Subhuman is more like it," Terry said.

"Speaking of my partner, by now he should be my ex-partner. So it's time to move on."

"What are you going to do?" Terry asked. "You obviously don't intend to be on the train when the bomb goes off. That chopper I saw on the flatcar—?"

"Exactly," said Deakins. "My ticket out of here. Wanna know where to?"

"No."

"A little cabin in the mountains, to start. Lovely place. Nice view, no gnats. When we get there, I'll make two phone calls. The first one's to the Pentagon. I'm gonna tell them where the train is." He grinned. "Some one-star will scramble a few F-16s down here, but by then the train will be on the outskirts of Vegas. I'll remind them about the impact trigger. If they hit the train or try to derail it, the nuke'll blow."

"And they can't stop the thing," she said, indicating the levers.

"No," said Deakins, "they can't. Not in time."

"You said two phone calls," Terry said.

"Right." He touched his head with his free hand. "The mind's going. Too much work for a non–type A like me. The second call's to my bank in Geneva. If I see big bucks in my account, I punch a few numbers on this." He slapped a leather pouch strapped to the side of his belt. "A remote shuts the timer and I leave the country. If not, half a million people turn into a warm evening breeze, along with my commander in chief. Which wouldn't be the worst thing in the world."

Terry said, "But I thought all the radio communications got fried. How will you—"

"Detonate the bomb?" Deakins said. "Very good question. Microwave. It's not affected by EMP. Perhaps you saw the dish on the roof?"

"I saw it," she said.

"So you see," said Deakins, "I really have worked this whole thing out, don't you think?"

"I hope you don't expect me to applaud."

"No," Deakins said.

He suddenly turned and pressed the gun to her temple. Terry briefly considered trying to knock it away. But with her hands on her head, the only way she could hit it was down. That would still put a burst in her side or leg.

"I do expect you to do something else, however," he said.

Terry's eyes craned to the side. She watched his finger on the trigger.

"I could live with taking out the President," Deakins continued. "I didn't vote for the dude, didn't like him when he was a senator. But half a million real people is a lot to carry on one's conscience. I'm not, as you put it, 'subhuman.' So I'm not going to arm the nuke."

"You're not?" she asked hopefully.

"No." He leaned closer and whispered, "You're going to do it for me."

56

As she crawled along the outside of the engine to the first car, Terry briefly considered jumping from the train. Assuming Deakins didn't plug her, maybe she could find a cave, or a hole, or a rock to hide under. Maybe she wouldn't be disintegrated with the rest of the city.

But her conscience wouldn't let her do it. Not as long as there was a chance that she could do something to stop Deakins.

All this death so one man could make some money, she thought. What was missing from his gene pool? Where did it all go wrong for him?

They made their way through the boxcars to the last one, Deakins following three feet behind Terry, his gun pointed at her head.

Even before they entered, Terry could smell the chicken shit. She walked in, saw the crates, the bomb, and the men. And realized it wasn't just the chickens that smelled.

"Gentlemen," Deakins said, "I'd like you to meet a very industrious park ranger." He poked the gun into Terry's lower back. "Introduce yourself to my team, please."

"Up yours," she said.

"Thank you," Deakins said. "Come with me, Ms. Yours. Or

may I call you by your first name? I feel as though we've known each other for quite some time."

Legs wobbly, Terry walked to where Deakins pushed with the gun. To where the bomb hung three feet from the floor of the car. The ceiling creaked as it swayed gently in its sling. She stepped up to the keypad.

"Start inputting, Up," Deakins said. "Nine . . . six . . . pound sign."

Terry repeated as she punched, "Nine, six, pound sign."

The numbers appeared in red on the display.

"Good," Deakins said. "Now, seven . . . star button . . . one."

Terry typed and said, "Seven . . . star button . . . one."

"Now hit Enter," Deakins said, "and you're done."

Terry stood there, staring at the keypad. She imagined that it was a touchtone telephone—the house phone in a hotel lobby. A lobby in Las Vegas. People checking in, taking tours, heading to a chapel to get married. She saw porters, cabdrivers, their families, their schools, their grocery stores. The images began to run, like a watercolor in the rain, and then there was only bleached whiteness growing brighter and brighter until it was blinding.

"Enter," Deakins said. "Do it now."

Terry extended her finger. She touched Cancel. The display went blank.

Deakins sighed. "You really shouldn't have done that."

"I'm dead either way," Terry said, "so fuck you."

"Well, yes," Deakins said. "It's difficult to argue with that." With a snarl, he grabbed a fistful of Terry's hair and pulled her closer. "There are good ways to die and bad ways to die. Good, for instance, might be getting nuked to atoms. Bad might be getting chopped up under the wheels of a speeding train." He looked at Sheppard. "Open the door."

Sheppard cocked a thumb at the sliding door on the side of the car. "This one?"

"Yes, that one!" Deakins snapped. "Up Yours is about to be Oscar Mayered."

Setting his gun down, Sheppard threw the lock switch and pulled back on the handle. He hesitated and looked back. "Boss, I don't know about this. She's a lady."

"A lady who killed your friend Max," Deakins said. "Now, open it."

Sheppard looked at her. "You killed Max?"

Terry said nothing.

"Man, you are not any kind of a lady," Sheppard said as he yanked the handle.

The door rolled open and, standing behind her, Deakins pushed the stumbling Terry toward it.

"Good night, honey," the major said as sunlight poured in—along with a sound that wasn't created by the train.

Deakins looked out at the roar and saw the helicopter rotor churning right outside the door. His eyes narrowed as he saw Hale. The captain was kneeling in the open hatchway, an automatic trained on the boxcar door.

"Let 'er go!" Hale yelled. "Now!"

Deakins wrapped his left arm around Terry. He hooked his right arm around her as well, and with his right hand pushed the muzzle of the automatic against the soft flesh under her chin.

"Fly away, little man!" Deakins yelled. "Fly away now or she dies!"

"Captain, take him out!" Terry yelled. *"The bomb's in this—"*

"Bitch!" Deakins snarled and pulled the trigger.

57

Terry once asked her jujitsu sensei what to do if someone were about to shoot at her. And Master Li replied, "Let them. Just don't be there when they do."

When Deakins screamed at her, Terry knew her time was up. So she dropped her right shoulder to throw him off-balance. Then she hooked her left foot behind his left knee and pulled in, while simultaneously pushing his right thigh back with her right hand.

He fell back with Terry on top of him, the gun spitting wildly to the right. One of the gunmen was hit in the neck and lay gasping for breath. Deakins was winded and his hold on Terry was broken by the fall. She rolled from on top of him and, scrambling to her feet, bolted for the door.

Hale watched as she swung out, reached for the ladder to the right of the door, and began to climb.

"That's my lady," he said as he got Deakins back in his line of fire.

Lying on his butt, Deakins also had Hale in his front sight. The two men opened fire.

Bullets chewed up the floor of the boxcar and the side of the helicopter. Hale ducked back into the cabin and Deakins rolled to the front of the boxcar. A moment later, the train door rolled shut.

Hale slung the gun around his shoulder and went back to the doorway. Terry was hanging on to the second-to-lowest rung of the ladder, trying hard to get her foot up.

"She's never gonna make it," Hale said to Wilkins. He turned to the pilot. "Get me closer."

"What are you going to do?" Wilkins asked.

"Try to get her in," Hale shouted as he got out on the runner. The chopper moved in.

"Closer!" Hale yelled back.

The helicopter moved closer, and Terry started to slip.

"Shit!" Hale yelled.

"She can't take the prop wash!" Wilkins cried. He leaned toward the pilot. "Pull away!"

"No!" Hale screamed.

He grabbed a coiled rope from the equipment rack and slung it around his shoulder. Releasing his grip on the side of the hatch, Hale swung his arms back, crouched, and leaped to the top of the train. He landed on his feet with a heavy thud then fell forward on to his knees. Turning, he crawled to the side of the train as the chopper moved away.

Hale looked down. Terry's mouth was taut, her eyes dark slits. She was struggling to hold on.

Working quickly, Hale made a lasso from one end of the rope—just as he had as a kid, back on the ranch. He lowered it toward her.

"Grab it!" he yelled.

She shook her head. "I—I can't let go!"

Terry's white-tipped fingers were beginning to slide from the rung. There was no time to waste. Hale put the rope down and climbed onto the ladder. Holding tightly with his right hand, Hale reached down and wrapped his fingers around the front of Terry's uniform.

"When I pull," he said, "let go and grab for the next rung, okay?"

She nodded. Emptying his lungs, Hale pulled hard on the intake. Inflating his lungs straightened his back and gave him extra leverage. As he tugged, Terry threw her hands up, kicked with her knees, and caught the rung. That gave her the extra height she needed to get her feet on the bottom rung. She hung on as Hale clambered to the top, and then she followed him up.

Hale looked into her eyes and put his hands on her arms. "Are you all—"

Before he could finish, bullets chewed through the roof of the car. Hale flopped onto his back and pulled her over him, shielding her. She rolled off him and away from the bullets, toward the satellite dish.

"Next car!" she cried. "There's no one there!"

Suddenly, one of the gunmen popped through the open hatch. He saw Terry behind the dish and smirked as he aimed his Stoner 63 machine gun at her.

A burst from Hale's automatic wiped off the man's smile along with the top of his head. Terry screamed as the white dish was splattered with his blood.

"Better him than you," Hale said as he reached Terry's side.

Hale crouched behind the dish, facing the hatch. He glanced toward the chopper, which was pacing the train some three hundred yards to the south and fifty feet up.

"I want to get you out of here," he said to Terry. "I'm going to motion the chopper over. When I do—"

A gun barrel poked over the top of the car, between the boxcar and the flatcar behind it.

"Get down!" Hale cried.

He got in front of Terry and fired at the gun barrel, which fired blindly. Bullets gnawed at the roof, just missing them as they hit the satellite dish and the hatch. Then bullets punched through the roof from below, just beside them.

"Come on!" Terry said, jumping to her feet and running toward the next boxcar.

He hopped up and followed her, zigzagging to avoid the bullets of the gunman between the cars. Hale looked back, firing as he ran, trying to keep whoever was back there from following them.

They reached the end of the car and Terry descended the ladder between the boxcars just as two men climbed up from the flatcar and another emerged from the hatchway, all of them firing. Returning their fire might have gotten one or two of them, but not all; instead, Hale followed Terry down.

As he reached the bottom of the ladder, she was standing on the coupling, trying the door of the next boxcar.

It was locked. Gunfire erupted from inside, forcing them toward opposite sides of the door.

Terry looked at the boxcar they'd just vacated. "Someone must have come through the bomb-car door on this side," she said, "entered the next car and locked the door behind them."

Hale nodded. He tried the door to the bomb car. It was locked.

"Deakins is probably still inside there with his precious bomb," Hale said.

He was looking intently at the boxcar and Terry knew what he was thinking. If they stayed here, they were fish in a barrel. If they went back to the roof, they were targets in a shooting gallery. But if they kicked in the door of the bomb car, they had a chance of taking out Deakins—even though they would probably die in the process.

Hale crossed the coupling to the door of the bomb car.

"Just so you know," Terry said, "this is a lot more than there was in my job description."

"I'm really sorry. I got you into this," Hale said.

"That's okay," she replied. "Just as long as one of us gets Deakins."

Hale looked at her with sadness, then alarm, as one of the gunmen stuck his weapon over the side of the boxcar.

"Get behind me!" Hale said, crossing the door to protect her with his body.

As he did, Terry braced herself to be shot at. And then she heard a sound that made her heart beat faster.

The sound of bad guys shouting.

58

When Hale jumped to the train, Colonel Wilkins ordered the chopper back. His plan was to follow behind the train until Hale and Terry were both safely on top, then move in and evacuate them.

When the gunmen emerged from the boxcar with their assortment of machine guns, rifles, and handguns, Wilkins held back. Any one of those weapons would have been enough to bring down the chopper or its occupants.

But when Hale and the ranger became trapped between the cars, Wilkins forgot about the chopper. He saw two brave Americans in danger and intended to help them. His determination was bolstered when Giles, Mr. ROTC Looey, sat in front of him swearing through his teeth like the Little Engine That Could.

"I want those fucks, I want those fucks, I *want* those fucks!"

"Then let's get them," Wilkins said.

The colonel gave instructions to the pilot, and the helicopter roared forward, diving toward the train. The chopper flew alongside it, level with the roof, the rotor blades spinning across the top of the cars. Screaming, the gunmen dropped to their bellies or dove for the hatch. None was killed, but none of them fired, either.

Reaching the end of the bomb car, the helicopter did a one-eighty on a dime and sped back.

As it did, Wilkins saw the side door of the boxcar slide back. Deakins was standing there, his legs spread wide, an M3A1 submachine gun tucked under his right arm.

"Pull away!" Wilkins screamed as Deakins opened fire.

His warning came too late. The .45-caliber bullets smashed through the glass and metal of the cockpit, chewing their way back, tearing into the pilot's left leg and Wilkins's shoulder.

"Christ!" Wilkins screamed, and slumped to the right. He clapped his right hand high on his left arm.

Giles leaned toward the pilot, who was leaning to the left. Chan's mouth was pulled tight and he was growling.

"Captain Chan, are you all right?"

"No!" he screamed.

The pilot's right hand was still on the control stick, his left on his bloody thigh. His eyes were on the shattered window. There were split cables and a sparking panel in front of him. The tail rotor was shifting slowly from side to side.

"We've lost rear lateral control," the pilot groaned. He fought to keep his eyes open. "I've got to set her down."

As he swung the chopper away from the train, Giles turned to the colonel.

"How badly are you hurt?" he asked.

"I'll live," he said.

The chopper listed dangerously to the left.

"Maybe," Wilkins added as Captain Chan righted it.

Biting his lower lip now, the pilot set the helicopter down on an uneven patch of desert. Scrub and tumbleweeds spun through the air as he shut down the rotor.

"There's a first aid kit behind the weapons rack," the pilot said to Giles.

"Right," Giles said. He squeezed between the seats to get it.

Wilkins lay back in the seat, listening to the train recede. He was breathing slowly and trying to eat the pain. In all his years in the military, which included combat in Panama and Desert Storm, this was the first time he'd been shot. It didn't feel the way he'd thought it would. He'd always been told that when the body was wounded, it went into shock. That the nerves shut down, that it wouldn't hurt as bad as you'd think.

That was bullshit. It hurt like deep, red hell. He felt as though someone had pinched his shoulder muscles with a pair of pliers and was twisting slowly. Every time he breathed or moved, bolts of pain shot down to his left heel.

He poked his middle finger into the hole, could actually feel the blood pumping against it.

"Hurry up, Giles," he said. "I'm going to bleed to death here."

"Coming," Giles said as he sat beside Wilkins and opened the kit.

Wilkins looked at the pilot. He was pressing his palm to his thigh and looking at the controls. "How are you, Captain?"

"Leg stings like a mother, but I'll live."

"Good man," Wilkins said.

Giles opened the colonel's shirt and placed a bandage on the wound.

"What kind of shape are we in?" Wilkins asked the pilot.

"Down but not out," Chan said. "If Mr. Giles would pass me a tourniquet, I can put my leg back together." He held up a broken wire. "Then I can put a few of these back together and get us airborne."

"Do it," Wilkins said to Giles. "To quote a friend of mine, 'I want those fucks.'"

59

When the helicopter retreated, Hale told Terry to bend and cup her hands. She did, and he placed his boot in her palms. Vaulting to the roof of the bomb car, he raced ahead, zigzagging to avoid being an easy target.

There was only one gunman left on top of the car. He was climbing to his feet as Hale rushed him. The men collided and the gunman fell back, off the end of the boxcar. He landed head-first on the flatcar; Hale fell on top of him, inadvertently bending the man's neck so the back of his head touched between his shoulder blades. There was a sound like popping bubble wrap and the man lay still.

Hale rose, wincing. He leaned against the chopper's sponson support strut as Terry came around the side of the boxcar. She stepped onto the flatcar.

"You all right?" she asked.

"I think I broke everything."

"You'll live," Terry said. She reached down, took the man's pistol, and tucked it in her belt. "At least you're not as bad as him."

"No," Hale agreed. "I broke him worse. Didn't mean to, though."

"Yeah? Well, get that 'I'm sorry' look off your face," Terry said. "It couldn't be helped."

Hale looked back at the bomb car. "Did you see who shot at the chopper?"

Terry shook her head. "I came around the other side. It was probably Deakins, though. He's not going to leave his pet bomb."

There were voices atop the boxcar and Hale looked up. He saw heads and gun barrels.

"They're coming back for another round," he said. "Let's go."

"Where?" she said. "We're running out of time!"

"I know," Hale said. He took Terry's hand and pulled her toward the tail of the Red Cross helicopter. "But if we're dead, it won't matter *how* much time we have."

As they ran along the chopper cabin, a gunman jumped from the bomb car to the flatcar. The thug fired, but the sponson was in the way and took the hit.

Hale and Terry kept running. Hale leaped over the cable holding the tail pylon to the car; Terry looked back at the gunman, didn't see it, and tripped.

Hale turned and helped her up just as the gunman came around the helicopter.

"Don't move!" the gunman yelled. He was holding his semiautomatic in front of him, at arm's length and chin high.

Hale was facing him. Terry's back was to him. Neither of them moved.

"Raise 'em!" the gunman said.

Hale did, slowly.

"You, too, chickie," the gunman said.

Terry scowled but obliged. As she did, she looked down at her waist. Hale followed her eyes and nodded.

A man yelled from the top of the bomb car, and Hale looked

up. The man had a Stevens Model 77 pump shotgun leveled at them.

"Get out of the way, Stempel," the man shouted. "These two are mine!"

"Aw, gimme a break, Sheppard!" the gunman yelled without turning. "Why can't we split 'em?"

"Because the lady killed my partner Max," said Sheppard, "and the guy thinks he's hot shit. So step aside."

The gunman scowled, still hesitating.

Hale looked at Terry. "When I move, fall flat," he said. Then he reached for her belt. Hale grabbed the pistol she'd taken from the dead gunman and, pushing her behind him, he fired at the gunman on the flatcar. The man twisted and fell. His gun skidded toward the chopper.

"Shit!" Sheppard yelled. He unloaded the shotgun at the flatcar. It punched a cloud of splinters several yards into the air.

But neither of his targets was where they had been. Terry was on her belly and rolling toward the chopper. After shooting Stempel, Hale had thrown himself sideward and was already behind one of the main undercarriage wheels.

Sheppard pumped another round into the chamber. "You're gonna die, asshole," he screamed, "wearin' big, ugly holes!"

Terry wriggled under the chopper to Hale's side. "How're we doing?" she asked.

"He says we're gonna die," Hale said.

"I don't think so," Terry said, and whispered something into Hale's ear.

A moment later, Hale yelled to Sheppard. "Hey, tough guy. You gonna shoot up the chopper?"

Sheppard sneered. "Naw. Just you."

"Not from up there you aren't!" Hale taunted. "Looks like you'll have to come and get me!"

Sheppard walked to the south side of the boxcar. "You don't think I will?"

"Nope," Hale said.

With a grunt, Sheppard leaped down and began walking along the edge of the flatcar, circling the chopper.

"Notice something?" Sheppard asked. "You can't get me from where you are, flyboy. Wheels are in the way. But in just a second, your ass is gonna be in my gunsight." He laughed. "An' I see the babe creepin' around behind you. Soon's I waste you, I'm gonna put some extra holes in her cute ranger butt."

Hale poked his gun around the chopper wheel and fired. The shot went yards wide.

"Not even close," Sheppard yelled. He raised the shotgun to his shoulder. "Here," he said. "Let me show you how it's done."

Just then, Terry rose from behind the landing light fixture at the front of the chopper.

"No, let me show you!" she said as she fired a burst from the semiautomatic which had slid under the chopper. The bullets struck Sheppard in the throat, sending bloody filaments in all directions, like a spiderweb. His shotgun dropped to the flatcar and Sheppard fell back silently from the train.

"Nice," Hale said.

As Terry dragged the dead gunman to the side of the flatcar and tossed him over, Hale retrieved the shotgun then went to the cockpit of the Red Cross helicopter. He took a screwdriver from the tool kit, then went to the engine panel by the tail rotor. He unscrewed it, disconnected a wire, and let the end drop to the flatcar. Then he put the tip of the screwdriver against the bottom of the gas tank and drove it in with the heel of his hand. There was a hollow *p-chang*. He removed the screwdriver, punched a smaller hole on the side, and gas began *glug*ing from the bottom hole. He tucked the screwdriver in his pocket and joined Terry in front of the cockpit.

"Done?" she asked.

"Done," he replied.

"So Deakins is stranded," she said. She looked ahead. "Now all we've got to do is stop the train."

"And deactivate the bomb," Hale said, "which will be kinda tough without knowing the code."

Terry said, "Nine, six, pound, seven, star, one, Enter."

Hale looked at her. "That helps."

"I thought it might."

Hale was about to add that she was amazing, when Deakins and the rest of his men climbed from the hatch on top of the bomb car. Hale and Terry ran toward the boxcar, reaching the side as the men gathered on the roof.

60

Deakins followed the three gunmen onto the top of the train.

"We're running a little late," he said to one of the men. "Fire up the bird."

While the man ran to the chopper, Deakins squatted next to the hatchway and looked around.

"I heard the shotgun go off," Deakins said. "So where's Sheppard? And Stempel?"

Another of the men said, "They're supposed to be right here. Maybe they went to check out the caboose."

"Find them," Deakins said.

Deakins watched as the gunman hopped down and ran toward the helicopter. Something wasn't right. If Sheppard had punched Hale's ticket, he'd still be crowing about it.

Deakins shielded his eyes from the sun as he walked toward the side of the boxcar. He looked out at the flatcar, at the helicopter. He watched as the gunman reached for the ignition key, then saw the wire hanging from the engine panel. Below it was a pool shimmering in the light.

"No," Deakins said. Then he screamed, *"No!"*

But he was too late. The gunman turned the key. A spark

hopped from the frayed tip of the wire and the pool of fuel caught fire in a flash.

The gunman looked back, saw the flames ride the stream of fuel up to the tank, and barely had time to scream before the helicopter exploded. The tail boom was lifted up by the blast, smashing the flight deck hard against the floor of the flatcar. The drive shaft snapped at the concussion and the rotor head flew toward the bomb car, its four blades turning a cartwheel. When the tail crashed back down, it separated from the main body of the helicopter as the two halves of the vehicle were swallowed in black-and-orange flame.

The man in the chopper and the gunman running past vanished in the blast. The last remaining gunman on the bomb car had hit the deck, but Deakins stood his ground. Shards of hot metal struck his legs, neck, and forehead with BB-like force; the heat of the explosion singed his hair and eyebrows.

"Didn't I say 'No'?" Deakins said under his breath.

The speeding train created a twisting trail of smoke and streaking flamelets. As the blast subsided and the blaze consumed the wreckage, the gunman rose. There was panic in his eyes.

"Boss, we're trapped here now. We'll have to shut down the nuke."

Deakins was staring out at the roiling flames. "Hale did this."

The gunman looked at the major. "Maybe," he said. "But maybe he was killed in the blast."

"No," Deakins said. "He wasn't. I feel him here." He looked at the thug. "I want you to find him for me."

"Find him," the gunman repeated uncertainly. "Okay. Sure. Meantime, you're gonna go back down the ladder and disarm the bomb, okay?"

Deakins turned and walked slowly toward the hatch.

The gunman looked back. "You'll take care of it, won't you?"

Deakins raised his hand but said nothing as he disappeared into the boxcar.

61

When Deakins emerged from the bomb car, Hale and Terry had gone around the side to the forward coupling. While Terry crouched beside him, steadying him on the rocking train and holding the shotgun, Hale attempted to work the screwdriver under the coupler knuckle pin.

"Son of a bitch won't budge," he said. "Goddamn rust."

Hale's eyebrows were thick with sweat. He dragged a sleeve across them, then bent, dug at the head again, slipped, and stabbed his hand.

"Shit!"

"You know what?" Terry said. "I'm going to go ahead a car and try the coupler there. You get to the bomb."

He nodded and handed her the screwdriver. "You're pretty good at memorizing numbers, aren't you?"

"You mean," she asked, "did I remember the code right?"

"Yeah," Hale said. "That's what I mean."

"I remembered it right," she said. "Have you?"

He nodded and they stared at each other for a moment. "In case something happens," Hale said, "I wanted you to know—"

"Save it," Terry said. "You'll tell me later." She slid a corner of the screwdriver head under the pin. *"Go!"*

Hale impulsively kissed her on the forehead, then rose, took the shotgun from her, and crossed the coupling to the boxcar.

There were three ways into the bomb car and, by his reckoning, there were only two men left—Deakins and one of the gunmen. Though that didn't exactly give him an advantage, it would be a good idea to enter where and when they might least expect it. He decided the hatch on top would work best. He could drop in, roll and fire, and be guaranteed to hit something unfriendly.

As he climbed the side ladder, he thought, *What I wouldn't give for a flash/bang grenade. I could take the pair of them out in a storm of light and noise.*

Upon reaching the roof of the boxcar, Hale noticed that the men had opened the side door. Hale guessed that Deakins didn't want any more surprises, like a chopper pacing him.

Too bad, Hale thought. *You got one more surprise coming.*

Hale was feeling confident that he could stop Deakins. He had the "big mo"—momentum—though as he crawled toward the hatch, he reminded himself that surprise notwithstanding, it was still two guys against one.

As he approached the hatch, he saw the rope he'd used to try to snag Terry. The lasso beckoned.

Setting the shotgun down, Hale slipped the lasso around the satellite dish, then squatted and made a noose from the other end, something he could put his foot in. As Hale finished the knot, he saw movement on the far side of the boxcar, near the flatcar. He looked over as the gunman came over the side.

Crouching on top of the car, the gunman reached for the semiautomatic slung over his shoulder. Hale's shotgun was on the other side of the satellite dish. There was no way he could reach it in time.

Hale's life didn't pass before his eyes, but fear did seem to heighten his senses. He heard the wind rushing past his ears, smelled the charred remains of the helicopter, saw the gunman's weapon come around in what seemed like slow motion. He felt the weight of the heavy rope in his hand, felt the scratchy fibers against his palm.

And then his hand moved. Faster, it seemed, than the hand of the gunman. The rope went out like a whip, snapping across the top of the train. It struck the gunman waist-high, and to keep from falling off he had to let go of the gun and grab the ladder.

The semiautomatic spun away from him, skidded across the top of the train, and dropped over the side.

Now there was only the shotgun, and Hale dove for it. So did the gunman, who used the handrails of the ladder to fling himself forward. Hale landed on his belly, on top of the gun, but the gunman landed on top of Hale. The thug seized Hale's hair and pulled back. Hale screamed, flipped over, and managed to throw his attacker off. The gunman rolled to the side, rose, and ran at Hale again, roaring.

Hale didn't have a chance to get the shotgun. But he was able to reach the rope and, climbing to one knee, he threw the noose toward the gunman's neck. It landed squarely as the gunman reached him. Flopping onto his back, Hale bent his legs, planted his feet in the belly of the onrushing gunman, and flipped him over his head.

The gunman landed on his back and slid toward the side of the boxcar. He tried to pull the noose from around his neck, but it tightened as he sledded down the gently sloping roof. The other end of the rope was still looped around the satellite dish. He went over the side and the rope went taut with a sickening *thwang*.

Hale had crawled back to get the shotgun. There wasn't time to think about whether or not he felt bad for the guy, who was probably still strangling down there. Hale had Deakins and twenty kilotons of nuclear weapon to worry about. He was willing to bet his old partner hadn't dropped what he was doing to cut his man down.

246

With the shotgun in his right hand, Hale walked toward the side of the boxcar and peered over. He was right. The gunman was kicking slightly, very slightly, as he hung in the open door. And then he stopped moving, except to twist in the wind as the train rushed ahead.

Turning around and dropping to his knees, Hale grabbed the rope in his left hand and took a moment to contemplate the grotesqueness of what he was about to do. On the other hand, it was probably the most self-sacrificing thing this gunman had ever done.

Taking a deep breath, Hale leaned back and did a makeshift rappel over the side.

62

As he watched the train vanish over the horizon, Colonel Wilkins felt as though he'd let his country down.

He was sitting in a vehicle that belonged in a used chopper lot, his arm throbbing painfully when he didn't move, and even worse when he did. They were the only salvation in the neighborhood, and he'd blown it. He'd let them get shot from the sky. What he should have done was forgotten about the ranger and concentrated on getting the bomb. That would have been the responsible thing . . . the right thing.

But she was in trouble, he tried to tell himself. Besides, with hindsight it was always easy to know what to do.

Giles was loading the guns, optimistically anticipating another crack at the train.

"Giles," Wilkins said weakly. "Load some of those." The colonel jerked his thumb toward a red box bolted to a shelf.

Giles turned around and opened the box. He removed bullets the size of Magic Markers and examined one closely.

"What are they?" he asked.

"Incendiary shells," Wilkins said.

"I thought we can't hurt the bomb," Giles said.

"We can't," Wilkins agreed. "But if we can get Deakins and his people off the train, maybe we can stop it."

"Gotcha," said Giles, who began removing shells from some of the guns and loading the new shells.

Wilkins was watching him. "Can I ask you something, Giles?"

"Of course, sir."

"When you were at Yale—did you get to do a lot of shooting?"

Giles flushed. He looked down. "No, sir. Most of our ROTC training was theory. Battle tactics, ethnic sensitivity in command, that sort of thing."

"I see." Wilkins said. "Well, just so you know, it's not complicated, really. All you have to do is point and pull the trigger. The gun does the rest."

"I think I can handle that." Giles smiled.

Wilkins returned his smile, then lay back and shut his eyes. He envied Giles the busywork, not to mention the hope. Having either of those right now would have made Wilkins a happier man. Instead, there was nothing to do but fight the pain and wait. Wait for Captain Chan to finish rewiring the damaged panel . . . or for the flash that would incinerate them all.

Damn fucking Deakins, he thought. The people entrusted with nuclear weapons were tested inside and out. Psychological profiles, background, friends, politics, every damn thing. How the hell had that waffle gotten in the stack?

What bothered him most about dying was all the people who would be going with him. That, and the fact that he'd have a moment between the time of the detonation and the arrival of the destructive pressure wave to reflect on his failure. He only hoped that that explosion they'd seen on the train was Deakins's helicopter. It'd be gratifying if goddamn Deakins boiled in his own atomic juices.

Captain Chan's voice pulled Wilkins from his reverie.

"I think I've got it," the pilot said, examining a connection. The smooth-faced young airman sat up and examined the panel. "Yeah, that should do it."

"Good work," Wilkins said.

The colonel sat up in his seat and sucked air through his teeth as pain shot from his arm to his neck and down his side. Chan didn't look quite as pained as he turned the key and fired up the main rotor. He looked wary and concerned, like a kid waiting to get his report card.

There was a loud, discouraging pop.

"That sounded like a light," Chan said, "blown by a power surge—"

Then there was a healthy chugging sound from somewhere above, followed by a gentle whirring as the rotor began to turn.

"Looking fine," Chan said as he moved the throttle and glanced from gauge to gauge. "Looking real fine."

The *chunk-chunk-chunk* of the drive shaft built quickly and Chan gave his passengers a thumbs-up.

"We're flyable," Chan said.

"Then let's go," Wilkins said, sitting up taller. His arm didn't seem to hurt as much as it had before. "I still want those fucks."

63

The legs of the hanged gunman were leaning slightly toward the rear of the boxcar, blown by the wind of the rushing train. He was twisting slowly counterclockwise, sending a thickening knot up the top of the noose.

Descending the rope, Hale grabbed the dead man's shoulders and slid behind him. His weight caused the corpse to stop twisting. Putting his foot against the side of the door frame, Hale kicked off. The body swung away from the train, like a pendulum, then back toward the open door.

Deakins fired two shots from his rifle and blood squirted from the gunman's chest. But the body protected Hale, who dropped to the floor of the boxcar when the corpse swung inside. He landed awkwardly and lost his shotgun upon impact; there wasn't time to recover it as he rolled to the rear, behind a stack of crates. By the time Deakins had aimed and fired again. Hale had crept behind the bomb.

"Now *that* entrance was what I call first-class rope-a-dope!" Deakins yelled. "Really well played, Hale, except that you put yourself in a corner!"

He walked toward Hale, firing at him and laughing as bullets clanged from the metal exterior of the bomb. Several hammock straps were severed and the bomb slumped toward the wall. Then the fusillade stopped as the rifle clicked on empty.

With a snarl, Deakins spun the rifle like a baton, then grabbed the barrel in both hands.

"Oh well," the major said. He hurled the rifle from the open door. "Guess I'll have to kill you the old-fashioned way. Beat you to a pulp."

"Goddammit Deak, it's over!" Hale cried. "I won. You lost. Deactivate the bomb!"

"Whoa, Nellie," Deakins said. "If it's over and I've lost, then how come the bomb's still ticking? I assume the bitch gave you the code." Deakins stopped walking. "I'll tell you what. Come on out, pard. I'll give you a minute to input the code. Hell, I'll even repeat the sequence just to make sure you got it right."

Hale was perspiring heavily. Deakins had something lousy up his sleeve.

"Of course." Deakins laughed, "You're gonna need this, too."

Hale poked his head over the bomb as Deakins pulled the remote control device from the leather pouch strapped to his belt. He wiggled it over his head.

"And you'll need it soon," Deakins said. "While you were outside playing Tarzan, I set the bomb to go off in five minutes. That leaves about four minutes, I'd say."

"But you'll die, too!" Hale said.

"Jeez, nothing gets past you, Hale," Deakins said. "But I've committed treason, Captain. Way I see it, it's better to die here than in a prison with hooded assholes lethally injecting me."

"But the humanity, Deak. The people."

"Fuck 'em," Deakins barked. "What'd they ever do for us except bitch about us screwing their daughters or rattling their windows with supersonic flights? Or complain that they were paying too much in taxes for us to risk our lives. Fuck 'em, Hale. Fuck 'em in spades."

"No, Deak. There are a lot of good people—"

"No, there aren't. Everyone's out for themselves. Now, you're wasting time . . . time you don't have. So here's all you have to do. You can enter the code on the nuke keypad or on this remote, but you can only deactivate the bomb with the remote. Hit Cancel, Enter, and that's it. Of course, you have to get it first."

Deakins grinned, crouched, and set the device on the floor of the train.

"The twenty bucks I took from you yesterday says you can't." Deakins pulled the money from his pocket and slipped it under the remote. Then he rose and shut the sliding door, locked it. "What say, hero? It's come down to just you and me, bare knuckles. You up to it?"

Hale stood. As his eyes adjusted to the dark, he saw Deakins standing about two yards behind the remote; the major was smiling and his fists were raised, circling each other like tiny moons.

"Yeah," Hale said. "I'm ready."

He stepped around the swaying bomb and raised his fists. He leaned into his left arm, which was leading.

Deakins glanced at the timer on the bomb and his smile broadened. "Three minutes left. One round. Fitting, don't you think?"

"I think you're scum," Hale said. "That's what I think."

"Good," Deakins replied. "I'd hate to fight my last fight against a guy who didn't want me." The smile vanished. "So come on, tough guy," he said. "Let's see if you can take me."

64

After making her way around the oil drums, Terry began to work on the coupler between the flatcar and the next forward boxcar. The train slowed as it climbed a hill, and with less rattling Terry was able to work on the pin with greater precision. There was less rust on this coupler, and though the pin came up slowly, at least it was coming up.

For several minutes as she struggled with the coupler, all Terry heard was the clatter of the wheels and the rush of the wind. Then she heard the bass roar of a chopper and looked back. The Air Force helicopter was approaching from the northeast, ferocious and fast, accompanied by the *budda-budda-budda* of someone firing from the air.

With an oath, she turned back to the coupler pin and dug harder with the screwdriver.

"What the hell are you firing at, pea brains?" she muttered. "There's hardly anyone left but us chick—"

Suddenly the pin flew out and Terry fell backward. She landed on the flatcar in a sitting position, her back slamming hard against an oil drum.

"Ouch," she said belatedly.

Looking ahead, she watched as the boxcars and engine as they moved away from the rest of the train.

The *budda-buddas* came closer as the rear half of the train slowed. Terry turned and saw bullets rake the smoldering wreck of the chopper. Then she realized that the airmen weren't shooting at the occupants of the bomb car, as she had initially thought. They were firing at the oil drums.

"My God!" she said. They were trying to kill Deakins and get to the bomb.

Jumping to her feet, Terry ran around the drums toward the bomb car, her arms waving wildly.

"Don't shoot!" she screamed. "We can do this!"

But they couldn't hear her, and because she was on the opposite side of the barrels Terry realized they probably couldn't see her either.

Summoning what little energy she had left, Terry raced to the bomb car, her legs churning madly. She jumped onto the end ladder, hauled herself to the roof, and dropped flat as the first of the incendiary bullets struck the rearmost oil drum.

65

The explosion punched its way from oil barrel to oil barrel, building in fury as it rolled forward. The blast blew the metal drums up and ahead, like bottle rockets, and several of them landed on the rearmost boxcars. The old wooden cars caught fire and the blaze quickly spread toward the engine. Oil from a crashing drum coated the locomotive and ran toward the tank of diesel fuel slung beneath it, between the forward and rear truck frames.

The oil bubbled and caught fire; moments later the tank exploded, kicking the locomotive up, splitting it in two, and dropping each half on opposite sides of the track. The boxcar behind it was ripped apart, wooden slats and splinters flying in all directions, but the two blazing cars behind it remained on the track. When the engine exploded, the boxcars stopped, then began rolling backward down the track.

66

Smoke from the still-burning flatcar filled the bomb car, though Deakins seemed oblivious to it, as he'd been to the explosion itself.

Hale knew his partner. Nothing existed for Deakins now— nothing except Hale's destruction.

They were circling slowly, still staring at each other over their fists.

Deakins jabbed with his right and Hale jerked his head way back, causing Deakins to miss with a left hook.

"Nice move," Deakins said. "Thought you'd go left and I'd clock you."

Hale said nothing. He didn't want to do anything to break his concentration.

"It's different without gloves, isn't it, sport?" Deakins said. "Modern boxing is such a pussy sport. All that counts is scoring points. Well, pard, this isn't about scoring points. It's about—this!"

Deakins faked with a right. Not wanting to repeat the move he'd just made, Hale went left. Obviously anticipating that, Deakins jabbed with his left and caught Hale on the chin, snapping his head back violently.

"You're bleeding," Deakins said. "Good. Didja know that in the old fights, in the 1800s, there'd be so much blood that guys would slip and fall?"

Deakins caught Hale with a strong left uppercut that opened a gash along his jaw and on Deakins's middle knuckle. Hale staggered back several steps. Deakins remained where he was, on the other side of the remote control.

Shaking his head to clear it, Hale came back to Deakins and raised his fists. His ears were ringing and the left side of his jaw stung, but he was still alert. Alert enough to know that there were two minutes, five seconds left on the timer.

Deakins smiled wickedly. "Let's see if we can't get a little more of that red stuff running out of you, okay? You ready?"

Deakins faked with a right uppercut and jabbed left. Hale blocked it with his right, and jabbed a hard left to Deakins's chest. Deakins turned sideways, to the right, and the blow missed him.

"Nice try," he said, "and good thinking. You break a rib, you put a guy out of commission. Problem is, you have to land the blow for it to be effective."

Deakins began to dance as he circled the remote control.

"Used to be every fight went to a knockout," he said. "But too many fighters got hurt. You know what happens when you get knocked out? Your brain slaps the side of your skull." He drove his fist into an open palm. "*Wham!* Lights out."

Deakins moved in slightly.

"Here," he said. "I'll let you see what it's like."

Deakins stepped toward Hale with his right foot, drawing out a left hook; he jerked back to avoid it, then moved in with a left uppercut. But Hale saw it coming, ducked to his left, and while Deakins's left side was exposed he hit him in the belly with a left-right-left combination.

Deakins doubled over, and Hale hit him with a right uppercut that started from somewhere around his knees. The blow stood Deakins upright and sent him stumbling back, arms pinwheeling.

"Does it feel a little like that?" Hale asked.

Deakins didn't answer. Before he recovered, Hale stepped over the remote and hit him with a right uppercut that dropped him to the floor. When Deakins went down, Hale spun and scooped up the controller.

He quickly examined the device as he walked toward the bomb. The far side of the car had begun to burn, providing what little illumination there was. Sweat from his brow dripped onto the remote as he began punching in the code.

Hale stopped when he heard the *click* behind him. The reloaded rifle discharged and he dove to the ground, twisting awkwardly as he fell so as not to land on the remote. The shell punched a hole in the wall where Hale's head would have been.

"The challenger takes a dive," Deakins said through bloody lips. He leaned against a crate of clucking chickens as he peered through the smoke. "The crowd roars its disapproval. Feathers fly."

The major spit out a tooth, tucked the rifle against his shoulder, and fired again.

Hale rolled to the side, toward the bomb, as the bullet dug a fist-sized hole in the floor. He rolled behind the bomb, crouched, and continued inputting the code. Behind him was a rising wall of flame.

Nine, six, pound—

Deakins smiled weakly as he approached the bomb. "Now you're in the corner," he said, "on the ropes. Pretty dumb move, Hale."

—seven, star—

Deakins was standing beneath the open hatch, less than two yards from the bomb. He raised the rifle. "Eight seconds on the clock," he said. "Seven seconds, six—not a lot of time."

Hale knew that, and strained to see the numbers in the dark corner.

—*one, Enter*.

That was the code. Then he entered what Deakins told him, and hoped the bastard hadn't been lying—

Cancel, Enter.

The bomb beeped. Hale took a quick look on the keypad: the numbers were frozen with two seconds left.

Deakins snickered. "You did it, but big effin' deal. I'm going to blow your goddamn heart out and then restart the—"

"Like *hell* you are!" came the voice from above.

The men looked up as Terry dropped through the hatch, landed beside Deakins, and knocked him against the rear wall with a jujitsu kick.

"You *are* one cocky ass pain," she hissed.

Hale came from behind the bomb. Terry was already running to the side door.

"Come on!" she cried as she pulled it open.

Hale stopped and glanced at Deakins, who was struggling to get up. Terry jumped back and grabbed Hale's hand.

"There isn't time!" she yelled, tugging him forward. "The other boxcars—"

Even as she spoke, the car was filled with the deafening crash of the two backrolling boxcars as they plowed into the flatcar. The bomb car itself rocked violently, then seemed to move up, back, and over at the same time as the flatcar rammed into it. Deakins was tossed into a corner of the spinning car.

Hale was still looking back as he and Terry leaped from the door. Deakins was looking at him as well. There was no concession in his eyes, no remorse, only defiance as the collision sent the bomb snapping back like a piston. The tapered end slammed into Deakins's chest and kept going, pushing him through the wall and onto the flatcar behind.

Hale saw no more. He was looking ahead now, and for a

moment he felt weightless as he flew threw the air beside Terry. Then they hit the rocky slope and rolled over and over, sideways and backward, until they hit a patch of prickle bushes some thirty feet below. Though it hurt to hit the spiny thorns, it felt good to stop, not to have rocks poking them through flesh and bone.

As smoke and charred debris poured down on them, Hale looked to his left. He saw Terry leaning on her forearms, facedown, spitting out dirt.

"You okay?" he said.

She looked at him. Her cheeks and chin were charcoal-black, her hair tangled among thorns. Her left pants leg was shredded from the knee down, and her shin was bleeding.

"Great," she said. "But next time, how about just dinner and a movie?"

Hale reached out and took Terry's hand, then lay back and listened to the crackle of flames, the distant beat of the helicopter, the silence of the dead train. He thought about Deakins and still couldn't believe what had happened. His friend, his copilot, the man he had trusted most had betrayed him. Had betrayed his country. What could he believe in after this?

Hale's dour reflections ended when he saw a singed twenty-dollar bill fluttering toward him. He rose and helped Terry extricate herself from the bush. Then he snatched the money before it could hit the ground and tucked it in his breast pocket.

Awful feelings aside, Hale knew he'd earned this one.

The chopper had been circling the wreck, and now it made a pass over Hale and Terry. Hale waved to them, and Captain Chan waved back. He indicated that he would land on a flat stretch up ahead.

Terry made a face.

"First they almost knock us off the train," she said, "then they try to blow us up. I think maybe we ought to walk home."

Hale rubbed his thumb across the dirt on her chin. Then he held her cheeks in his hands. "I've had survival training. Maybe we ought to camp out here for a few days."

"I think I'd be safer in the chopper."

"Probably," Hale admitted.

"I also think you should get all your cuts and bruises tended to," Terry said. "Besides, we've never even been properly introduced."

Hale smiled and drew his shoulders erect. He extended his hand.

"Reilly Hale," he said.

She took his hand. "Terry Carmichael. Pleased to meet you."

Hale held on to her hand as they turned and began walking toward the helicopter.

"Just out of curiosity," he said, "what kind of food do you like?"

"Sushi," she said. "I like it so much I'm learning Japanese. You?"

"I like my fish cooked. Blackened, Cajun style."

"Ecch," she said. "What about movies?"

"Action," he said. "Especially Hong Kong. Ringo Lam, Ronny Yu, those guys."

"British," she countered. "Lots of meaty dialogue."

"Right," he said. "And let me guess. You only watch PBS on TV."

"No—"

"Thank God," he said.

"When I have free time, I read."

Hale frowned. "I don't suppose Clancy—"

"The Brontës," she said. "Austen."

"You care for sixties rock?" Hale asked, his spirits sinking.

"Classical."

"Beaches?"

"Museums."

262

"Sex?" he asked hopefully.

She looked at him. "Yeah," she replied. "A whole lot."

"You mean, you like it a lot or you like a lot of it?"

"Both," she said.

Hale hugged her around the waist and smiled broadly. "So who'll have time for all the other stuff?" he teased as Giles came running toward them and Wilkins gave them a thumbs-up from the chopper and Hale realized that, with any luck, he'd have something very special to believe in.

THE
X-FILES

WHIRLWIND

*A novel by Charles Grant based on
the characters created by Chris Carter.*

Unnatural disasters . . .
Serial killers come in all shapes and sizes. But this one is
particularly puzzling. There's no pattern to the muti-
lated bodies that have been showing up in Phoenix:
both sexes, all races, ages, ethnic groups. There is no
evidence of rape or ritual. Only one thing connects the
victims, the natural disaster that killed them. One of the
most unnatural natural disasters imaginable, leading to
a most painful, most certain and most hideous death . . .

'The series remains one of the most slickly produced
hours on television, notable for its cryptic endings, and
sharp, intelligent writing'   *Variety*

'The most provocative series on TV'
                                          Entertainment Weekly

0 00 648205 8